~ TALES FROM THE ~

# Haunted Mansion

Autumn
Publishing

Published in 2019
by Autumn Publishing
Cottage Farm
Sywell
NN6 0BJ
www.igloobooks.com

GRA005 0319
2 4 6 8 10 9 7 5 3 1
ISBN 978-1-78905-834-5

Printed and manufactured in Italy

# TALES FROM THE
# Haunted Mansion

## VOLUME I
### THE FEARSOME FOURSOME

Transcribed by **John Esposito**
as told by mansion librarian **Amicus Arcane**
Illustrations by **Kelley Jones**

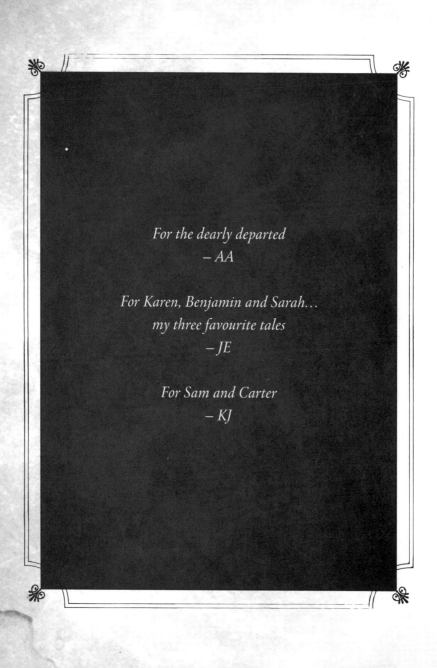

*For the dearly departed*
*– AA*

*For Karen, Benjamin and Sarah…*
*my three favourite tales*
*– JE*

*For Sam and Carter*
*– KJ*

# Welcome to Our Library

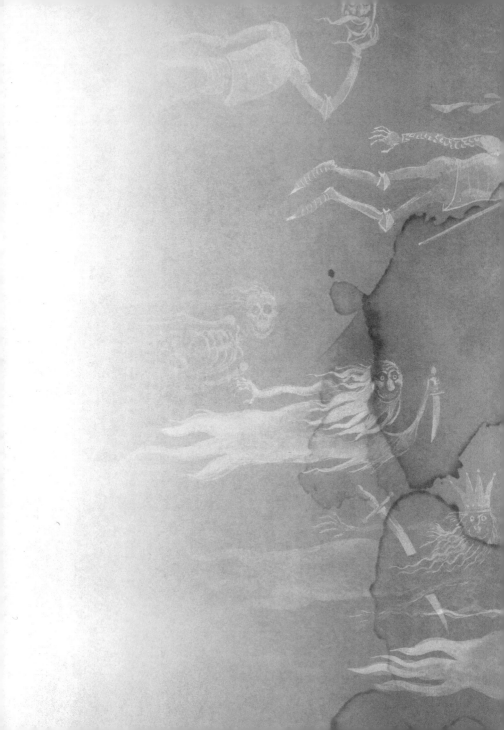

# STOP READING!

You heard me. Put this book down this instant.
Put it back where you found it!
For your own sake, I beseech you.
You're not the type.

What type is that, you ask?

Our type.

Still here? Very well. Can't say we didn't warn you.

Welcome, foolish reader, to the illustrious library of... well, you know where you are. Allow me to introduce myself. I am your guide, Amicus Arcane, the soul librarian and entrusted keeper of 999 bone-chilling tales. Every spirit has a story, you see: a haunted history dying to get out... so it can follow you home. But heed this warning: we're always on the lookout for one more tale.

Perhaps even yours.

We — if you haven't guessed — are known in the parlance of the living as spirits, spectres, poltergeists, apparitions. Or, if you prefer...

... ghosts.

We are at our most spirited amongst the books, harbouring a special affinity for those tales that burrow under the flesh, long after their authors have departed their corruptible mortal vessels. In this way, books themselves are rather like ghosts. Their very bindings contain the spirits of the dead. And that means this terrifying tome is haunted, which means this isn't merely a book you're holding, but an actual ghost. And that brings us to the subject at hand: the Fearsome Foursome.

Their little club, you see, was also interested in ghosts... and zombies and mummies and just about everything that goes bump in the night. Their founding body consisted of Willa, Tim, Noah and Steve, four middle school students with a talent for storytelling and an appetite for the macabre. Their one goal: to frighten the wits out of each other with the scariest stories they could muster. A lofty goal, if I may say so myself. But this week, their meeting was abruptly cancelled.

As it happens, their clubhouse was ravaged by a violent storm. Perhaps we had something to do with it. Who can say?

My memory isn't what it used to be since that doctor removed my brain.

The important thing to take with you is that the Fearsome Foursome had no place to tell their tales. So we provided them with a home. A bit off the beaten path, I will admit. But you can always take the shortcut through the graveyard.

It's almost time for you to meet them. You see, I too, have a tale or two or three or four that I'm dying to share. Once they heard them, their lives were never the same.

Nor will yours.

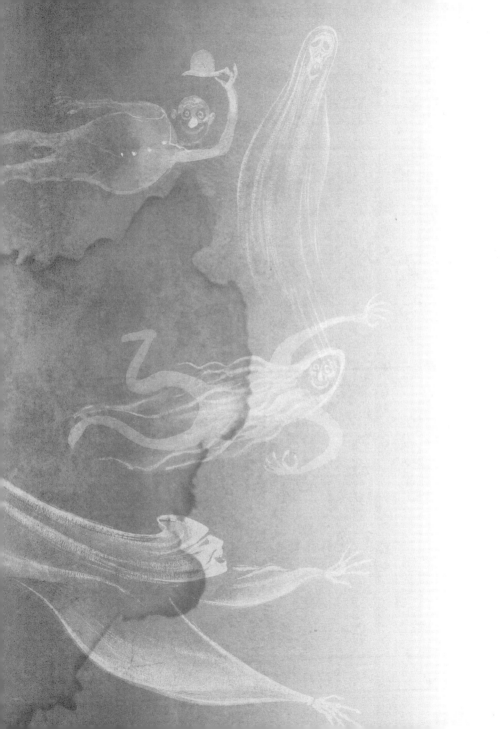

# Chapter One

## THE FEARSOME FOURSOME

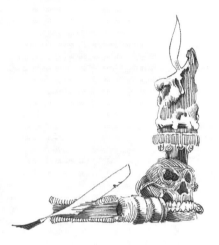

**I**t all began at a lunch table, where a good number of friendships are born. Willa was reading *Poe's Tales of Mystery and Suspense*, a dog-eared paperback containing classic stories written about a million years ago. The wording could be tricky, but once you got used to it, you'd be treated to the finest horror stories ever put to paper. More important, Willa was reading because she liked to read, not because it was assigned. And really, who reads any more? **Besides you, that is.**

Tim was passing the table, balancing a tray of what could generously be described as a macaroni item, when the cover caught his attention. It featured a black cat with a missing eyeball drooling something red. You know, one of those covers you can't take your eyes off of, or, in the case of that particular black cat, eye, singular.

Tim made a beeline for Willa. Maybe it was her book. Or her hair, which could best be described as 'seasonal'. Not the cut – the colour. Those days it was blue, matching Willa's eyes. Tim cleared his throat before opening with a compliment. "That is *so* sick."

Willa glanced up over her shoulder. "Excuse me?"

"I have the same book," he said, "only mine has a raven on it." Tim slipped his hand into a New York Yankees backpack and pulled out his copy of *Poe's Tales*.

Willa was momentarily impressed, until she spotted the word *abridged* under the title. "You got ripped off," she said. "'Abridged' means they cut things out. Usually the good parts, like when they show *Beast Feast* on TV. You need to get the uncut version." She went back to her Poe, not coincidentally, the uncut version.

But Tim hung around like a puppy, waiting for Willa to finish her page. Again, she glanced back. "May I help you?"

"My name's Tim." He extended his hand and Willa shook it, almost breaking it. She wasn't a tomboy or anything. She was just stronger. And faster. But not smarter. On that score, Willa and Tim were in the same league.

"Willa," she finally conceded.

Tim took the initiative, asking her if she knew his pals Noah and Steve. She'd heard of Steve, of course. Who hadn't? Steve had a reputation for being a bad boy, which he wasn't. But like it or not, looks went a long way in middle school. And Steve certainly looked the part.

Noah looked his part as well. He was a chubby redheaded geek she remembered from a recent science fair debacle: the banned *Dinosaurs versus Teachers* exhibit.

"They're really into horror, too."

She looked surprised. "Steve's into horror?"

"You wouldn't think so, I know. He's one of the cool kids." Willa shot him a look that suggested he was about to get decked. "Not that you're *not* cool!" he quickly added, fearing for his life. "Steve-o got me into Poe." He turned his paperback on its side, showing her Steve's name written in marker. "Noah's into Lovecraft. Ever hear of him?"

Willa nodded. "H. P. Lovecraft, the writer? Providence's own? Of course!"

Tim was bubbling with excitement. Or maybe it was the macaroni item. Let's just say *something* was bubbling in his belly. "We're starting a club. For horror lovers only. Right now, it's just the three of us. But there's always room for one more."

Willa instantly took to the idea. Horror lovers were in short supply those days. "You mean like a readers' circle?"

"More like a storytellers' circle." Tim leant in, suddenly serious. "We don't just read scary stories. We *invent* them."

That brought Willa to her feet. She was about three inches taller than Tim on a good day. It was a good day. "Scary's what I do!" she said. "I'm going to be a horror writer when I grow up."

**If you grow up, Willa. If!**

"Does that mean you're in?"

"Does a vampire drink blood?" she replied. Tim raised his hand for a high five, fearing a second handshake might send him to the hospital.

SLAP! *Ouch.*

They exchanged smiles, the first of many. Tim recognised her as one of his own. That's what a club is, after all: a group of people who like the same things you do. Not to mention Willa was a girl. One day he might recognise that, too.

During the walk home from school, Willa met with Noah and Steve for their approval. Their first order of business was coming up with a name for their club. After passing on Club Wretched and the Frightmare Fraternity, they officially settled on the Fearsome Foursome.

And every week after, barring sickness, funerals, holidays and funerals... **did I say funerals twice?** Willa, Tim, Noah and Steve gathered to exchange tales of ghosts, ghouls and graveyards. In no time at all, they became more than a club. They became like a family. A family of friends united by all things spooky.

That brings us to one particularly important night, about a hundred stories later. Thunder crackled and lightning flashed; it was a night tailor-made for tales that make you shiver.

Earlier in the day, their regular headquarters had been mysteriously demolished by a freakish storm. **Call it fate. Call it destiny. Call it a convenient plot twist.** In the place where it used to stand were four frighteningly fancy invitations, directing Tim, Willa, Noah and Steve to an address on the other side of town.

So they gathered after dark, carrying standard story-telling paraphernalia – torches, marshmallows and blankets – and made their way to the unwelcoming wrought-iron gate of a sprawling estate.

# THE FEARSOME FOURSOME

The gate itself was half open, as if they were expected, which they fully were. As they slipped through, Willa was surprised at the pristine condition of the grounds. There were no cobwebs or screeching rats or any of those unsightly accompaniments one usually associates with that sort of dwelling. However, the property did have its share of creepy delights…

Like the pet cemetery, which Willa spotted on a hill. That sent a shiver up her spine.

Directly after that, Noah pointed out a trio of stone enclosures resembling those hideous storage pods you see on people's lawns. These had drawers with coffins in them, a few still decorated with wilting flowers. Right away, Tim knew what they were. "Mausoleums. Dead people live inside those things."

Steve rolled his eyes. "That's an oxymoron, moron. Dead people don't *live* anywhere." He knocked on one of the drawers. "You up?" Noah half expected a response.

Willa elaborated, "Some people don't like the idea of being buried under the ground. In the old days, certain mausoleums even attached bells. In case you got buried alive, you could ring for help."

"Or for *tomb* service," Noah said, giggling.

Willa and Tim groaned. But not Steve. "That was so bad I won't even dignify it with a groan," he said.

Noah couldn't shake off the thought. The very idea made his skin crawl. "Buried alive. Eeeeh. That's a fate worse than death."

Steve considered it. "I don't know. I could think of worse."

"Like what?"

I could say, but that'd be telling, and I wouldn't want to do that. Not yet, anyway. You and young Steven will find out soon enough.

The Foursome continued up the winding path, where blackened branches hovered like the dying limbs of an ancient behemoth. Or, if you prefer, old tree branches drooped over their heads.

*Caw! Caw!* A large black bird – a raven, if you haven't guessed – was watching from one of the branches. Its head turned as they went by, as if the bird was passing judgement. Poor Steve. He had a queasy feeling, like he'd seen it all before. Somebody *always* feels like that in one of these stories. You thought so, too. Didn't you?

"Déjà vu," Steve whispered.

"Déjà who?"

"That's French for been there, done that." It was his best translation.

"My mom's learning French," said Noah, his cheery pronouncement met with complete and utter silence. No one cared. *Caw! Caw!* Well, except for the raven.

The others continued moving, but Steve lingered a bit longer, examining the landscape, the trees. It wasn't just that he felt he'd been there before. It was like he'd never left.

Willa arrived at the front door, the boys bunched behind her like three curious shadows. At precisely the same moment, all four heads looked up to see a mansion towering above them.

It was an imposing structure of a time and a place all its own, erected from brick and mortar and a touch of grand imagination. Its very design was a contradiction in styles; turrets jutted into the clouds like a centuries-old Gothic building, while stone columns adorned the entrance like something you'd see in an antebellum manor. What the Fearsome Foursome couldn't know was that the mansion looked whichever way they thought it should appear, as if it was some kind of phantom manor.

The front door was decorated with a wreath of dead flowers. Not a holiday wreath, unless you consider a funeral a holiday. Willa crossed over the threshold and entered the house, with the boys sticking close behind her. Instantly, the humid night air turned frosty. It was as if someone had cranked up the AC. (But let's get real. Ghosts don't do air-conditioning.)

She abruptly stopped and Tim slammed into her, something he did so often it was barely noticed. He heard something, a jingling noise he didn't recognise. It came from Willa's wrist. "Hey! What is that thing?" he asked.

She jiggled her arm – *jingle-jangle*. "It's not a thing, it's a charm bracelet. Why? Can't a girl wear jewellery if she wants to?"

"I guess. It's just... I never thought of you as a girl before."

Willa shot him a look, followed by a sharp elbow. "Why not?"

Tim coughed, winded. "Ugh... *that's* why not."

They moved forwards as a unit, arriving in a larger foyer. Willa moved her torch up and down the walls. The mansion was a morbid masterpiece of design. There were snakes for door handles and skulls carved into the moulding. Even the wallpaper had eyes! And yet the house was well tended. As Willa pointed out, there was nary a speck of dust, let alone a dirty sock. Noah silently disagreed, seeing layers of dust on the railing and cobwebs on the chandelier.

As the group moved forwards, Willa held her light on a luxurious fireplace. In the dark, it also appeared to have eyes. She dismissed it as an illusion, a trick perfected by the shadows.

Oh, I hate to break it to you, Willa, but our fireplace has eyes in the daytime, too. The better to see you with, as the saying goes.

Her torch continued crawling up the wall until... *Gasp!*—a face stared back at her. It was the portrait of a gentleman, a real old dude. Judging from his attire, he lived – that term's used loosely around here – a seriously long time ago. As a group, they guessed fifty years ago. Maybe even a hundred. Or last Tuesday. Art experts they were not.

"I'll bet he was the master of the house," speculated Willa. "The lord of the manor."

"He probably croaked here, too," added Steve. He pointed to the spot where Noah was standing. "I'd say in this very room."

*Gah!* Noah backed away, gobbled up by the shadows, and re-emerged... in the next corridor. The others followed, and as the darkness swallowed their lights, the portrait returned to its natural appearance, which was one of decomposition, for now there was a well-dressed skeleton, still possessing the master's eyes, in the oversized frame.

# CHAPTER ONE

You're thinking these were mere parlour tricks, hmm? Well, think again. The worst is yet to come.

The next stop was a portrait chamber of octagonal design. That's eight sides, must I do all the work here? A framed portrait hung on every other wall panel, resting below a domed ceiling. Perhaps those portrayed were former residents. But something else was bothering Noah.

"This place was supposed to be empty, right?"

Steve confirmed that was what the invitation said.

"Then who lit the candles?" Noah pointed at the wall sconces. They were shaped like gargoyles, each one clutching two lit candles.

And then something utterly bizarre for a book called *Adventures in Happyville* took place. But for one called *Tales from the Haunted Mansion*, it was not so unusual at all. The portraits began to stretch, changing the images from serene to sinister. The four didn't know if the pictures had elongated or if the whole room had stretched.

"How?" Tim asked. "How are they doing this?"

Willa and Noah took some guesses, but not Steve. He didn't care about the how. He was too busy looking for a way out. "Hey, guys, I hate to break it to you. We're not going anywhere! There are no windows and no doors."

Panic would have set in had Willa not been leaning against a false wall. Right on cue, it glided open to reveal a secret passageway. She couldn't resist embracing this magical moment. "There's always my way." Willa passed through the wall that was no longer a wall.

The others followed her through. Had they remained a second longer, they would have witnessed a series of lightning flashes flickering from the dome. And then they would have seen the figure of a man hanging by a noose from the rafters. But they had already moved on, so they were spared. Unlike you, foolish reader.

Now the storm had arrived, full force, and wouldn't be going anywhere for a while… just like our four friends. All bunched together, arms holding arms holding waists, eight legs moving as one like a human spider. As horror experts, they knew this was only the beginning.

One corridor led to another. A suit of armour stood guard by what could only be described as an endless hallway. And far down the hallway, a candelabrum seemed to float weightlessly. Before they could question what they saw, the candles winked out and they were ensconced in darkness once more.

Then Willa heard a distinctive sound. "Shhhhhh!" she hissed.

# CHAPTER ONE

Tim whipped his head round. "Why 'shhhhhhh'?"

"I heard music." Willa turned to Noah and Steve to see if they'd heard it, too. Like Tim, they hadn't. But they knew Willa well enough to believe every single word she said.

"What kind of music?" Noah asked. "Rap? R&B?"

"More like D&B. Dead and buried. It was an organ. Like you hear at church or a funeral." She aimed her torch into the hallway. "It came from down there."

"Down where?" Steve asked.

Indeed, the corridor appeared to have no end. It did, of course. It had to, right? But the idea made about as much sense as anything else around the place. Like the various staircases climbing up walls and across ceilings, leading to nowhere. Or the strange grandfather clock that struck thirteen. All they could do was keep moving. If there was a mystery as to why they'd been invited, that would be the only way to solve it.

The friends found themselves entering a quaintly decorated room, loaded with books from floor to ceiling, in cases and on shelves. Hardcovers, exclusively, of various colours and conditions: a collection that could only be built over time. It was the mansion's library, of course, absent any modern amenities you might find in your local library. **Unless** your local library happens to be located inside a haunted mansion, in which case I offer my sincerest condolences.

Almost immediately, Willa hopped onto the lowest rung of a ladder built on a sliding track, perusing the titles. "Guys, you're not going to believe this."

Tim walked under the ladder. "What'd you find?"

"These books. They're all ghost stories. Every single one of them."

Weird enough. But what happened next really chilled their blood. A disembodied voice boomed from the dark recesses of the room: "Our library is well stocked with priceless first editions."

Willa, Tim, Noah and Steve spun round to face… whatever it was.

A figure materialised from the shadows; a thin man with a lantern-shaped jaw, holding a candelabrum. He had an ashen complexion and wisps of white hair outlining his cheeks so that when he spoke, he resembled a talking skull. Which really shouldn't offend anyone. When you think about it, we're all talking skulls. "Welcome, foo —" He corrected himself. "Friends." His voice was gentle, almost soothing, but that didn't fool anyone.

Willa was quick to explain: "We're not burglars or anything. We thought nobody lived here."

"You're quite right," the talking skull confirmed. "No *body* lives here. Forgive me for creeping up on you. Old habits die hard." He was formally dressed, all in black, as if he was attending a wake – his own, of course. A crumpled carnation was still in his lapel.

He tilted his candelabrum, throwing both light and shadow onto a collection of exquisitely sculpted marble busts, of which he was justly proud. "You will recognise their faces. Marble busts of the greatest ghostwriters the literary world has ever known. They were commissioned by the master... before his untimely demise."

"Who are you?" asked Steve directly.

"I am the librarian," he replied. "I have always been the librarian."

"How long's 'always'?"

The librarian furrowed his brow. "I've never been very good with dates, but I do recall President Lincoln complimenting me on my spats. A fine gentleman, Mr Lincoln. Wonderful hat. Is he still in office?"

The others chuckled politely. Yet the librarian wasn't

joking. "Have I interrupted a meeting of some importance?" he asked.

"We're the Fearsome Foursome," replied Willa. "We tell stories. But not just any old stories. We only do scary."

Tim completed her thought. "The scariest one wins all the dessert you can handle. Usually ice cream."

Noah raised his hand. "I won six times!"

"No doubt," said the librarian with a nod. He reached for a book on the highest shelf. Again, it must have been a trick of the light, because the book seemed to glide down into his hand on its own. "It sounds like a most delightful endeavour. May I begin?" He blew dust from the old tome. "It's been forever since I tasted ice cream… and I have the scariest stories of all."

Willa's eyes lit up. "You do?"

Steve was growing impatient, and when that happened, rude was never far behind. "Go chase an ice cream van!" He turned to the others. "It's time to split."

The librarian clasped a hand over his mouth. "Oh my, I've frightened you."

"Fat chance, old man. It'll take a lot more than you've got!"

"But I've told you… I've got the scariest stories of all," the librarian replied.

But Steve wasn't giving in. "Oh, yeah? And what makes yours so scary?"

"My stories are about each of *you*."

There was a moment's hesitation as the four friends glanced at one another. Then Steve stepped forwards. "Nice try," he said defiantly.

The librarian smiled. "Then you'll have no objections if I begin on this side of the room." The librarian extended his finger, panning it across the library until it stopped. "Tim."

Tim gulped. "H-h-how did you know my name?"

Steve shook his head. "Because he heard Willa say it, like, two seconds ago."

But Tim knew different. **As do you.** "Master Timothy," continued the librarian, "are you ready to hear your tale?"

"What do you mean, *my* tale?"

"The first story is all about *you*. And that remarkable old glove you found."

A jolt of fear shot through Tim's body. He turned to Willa. "My baseball mitt. Lonegan's glove. How did he…"

Steve, ever the sceptic, replied, "He sees you're into baseball, Einstein. You're wearing a uniform!"

"Would you care to hear what else I know?" It was more a statement than a question, and before Tim could reply, the librarian was leafing through the introductory pages, his finger stopping on our first story, a tale known as...

# Chapter Two

## LONEGAN'S GLOVE

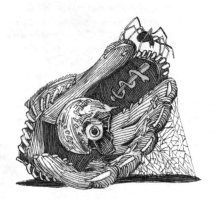

# I

t's America's national pastime. No, not grave robbing. *Baseball.* The national pastime is baseball, a game that, more often than not, rewards failure. Don't believe it? Consider this: a player with a .333 batting average, which means he gets out two out of three times he steps up to the plate, is hailed as a superstar. That's failing most of the time. And consider pitchers. They work every fourth game and aren't expected to hit at all! If they do, they're practically knighted for it. Crazy game, this national pastime. The perfect game. For Tim, that is.

Tim had a genuine love of the game. Before Poe and Lovecraft entered his world, there were Ruth and DiMaggio.

Tim could relay figures and spout stats till the teeth fell out of his skull. Or is it 'stars fell out of the sky'? No matter. He knew everything about the game, but that didn't help him in the one department he cared about most: *playing* the game.

Tim couldn't play baseball to save his soul.

Not that he didn't try. He'd joined Little League every year since he was seven. That was five seasons ago, and by now, he was on his way to becoming a professional benchwarmer. His mum tried putting it in perspective. "Worry about your grades," she said. "Maths and English skills pay bills."

True, true. But Tim was quick to point out, "When was the last time Derek Jeter had his electricity turned off?"

For Tim, the real trouble began on a Saturday in a place coincidentally called Amicus Field. Amicus. That's Latin for 'friendship'. But really, who speaks Latin any more? It's only good for reading. And we've already established that nobody reads any more... besides you, that is.

Tim liked to scour the local flea markets, looking for finds. That week he was accompanied by his best bud, Willa. Yes, *that* Willa, the cutie with the blue hair, only it was green the day this story took place.

As it happened, Amicus Field was hosting its biweekly flea market. By yet another coincidence, it had been the site of a baseball field, now long forgotten, where a gruesome tragedy had taken place. In real life, gruesome tragedies are rarely pleasant, but, oh, are they a hoot to read about! And let's face it... we wouldn't have a proper ghost story without one. And this is a proper ghost story. Now don't you fret, you'll get all the gory details... if you dare to keep reading.

As for Tim and Willa, they'd been hanging out a lot more since they both turned twelve, though neither one could tell you why. Okay, that's not entirely true. Willa could tell you why if she really had to. But that would require sounding like a girl, so why risk it? It was funny, because not so long before, those two had got along like blood and embalming fluid. Or is it oil and water? However that goes.

At the moment, Willa was nagging Tim to split so they could hit a local street fair. "They have live music. We could be dancing instead of wasting our Saturday looking at junk!"

"So who asked you to waste it?"

Willa got right in his face. "You want me to leave?"

"Be my guest."

He noticed something reddish on her cheeks and tried rubbing it off. For the first time, Willa was wearing make-up. "Just for that, I'm gonna stay," she said. "I'll be your worst nightmare."

"What else is new?" Secretly, Tim was happy she stayed, but he wouldn't dare let on. Why spoil the fun?

They passed a ginormous table loaded with used toys. Tim was a quick browser, spotting something he liked within seconds. In that case, it was a Major Jensen astronaut figure in excellent condition – well, except for the missing limbs. He held it up to the seller. "Excuse me. How much for the No Legs Major Jensen?"

*Good Lord*, thought Willa, *he knows its name*. She didn't know whether to deck him or kiss him.

"It's vintage!" confirmed the old lady behind the booth.

"Of course it is," Willa said.

Tim gave Willa a hip check. "Don't mind her. She's a non-believer. How much?"

"Shall we say… five dollars?"

Willa practically choked on her own tongue. "Shall we say… *that's insane*? Put it down, Timothy." She only used 'Timothy' when things got real. "Immediately!" Tim did as ordered, returning No Legs Major Jensen to the woman behind the booth.

In life, as well as the afterlife, we rarely know how one thing will affect another until it's too late. If Tim had bought No Legs Major Jensen, then maybe, just maybe, he would have passed up the infernal thing that caused all the trouble. And the horror. And the gore. And all that other stuff you're reading this book for. But then we wouldn't have a story. Certainly not one called 'Lonegan's Glove'. And let's face it… as titles go, 'No Legs Major Jensen' doesn't have the same ring to it.

Willa was already making the hard push for an ice cream when Tim spotted the item from way across the market. It called to him, like pink lemonade on a hot summer day. Off he went, with a confused-looking Willa lagging a few steps behind.

There it sat, surrounded by trinkets – none of which had anything to do with *the game*. It was a baseball glove, older than the hills. From the 1950s was Tim's guess, which was spot on.

"Nineteen fifty-five," confirmed the vendor, as if reading Tim's mind.

Tim looked up to see an elderly man dressed in denim overalls; a worn-out baseball cap perched crookedly on his scalp. Tim mustered the courage – yes, it took courage – to ask if he could have a look.

"You're already looking at it, young friend," responded the vendor.

Willa whispered in Tim's ear: "I bet it's vintage." She was teasing him, of course. But very soon the teasing stopped and even Willa would have thrown down cold, hard cash for it. Because she saw the look on Tim's face. The glove was already working its magic.

"You can hold her, if you'd like."

Tim picked up the glove like a child reunited with his first toy. It was large, probably an early outfielder's mitt, and, barring the rust-coloured stain near its heel, in terrific shape. It even had the original laces. And then there were the fingers themselves. Six, to be exact.

What drew Tim in, however, was its history. He recognised the markings on the pocket: the number thirteen and a tattoo of a snake coiled round a baseball bat. This left little doubt… it was Lefty Lonegan's glove!

Now for you non-fanatics wondering who or what a 'Lefty Lonegan' is, keep your skin on. If we told you now, it would spoil all the fear… I mean, fun.

The vendor recognised the look in Tim's eye. Or maybe it was the look of Tim's mouth: open like a fish's, ready to be hooked. "Try her on," he suggested.

A shiver rattled Willa, and not a girly shiver; this was her first true burst of women's intuition. Something wasn't right

# CHAPTER TWO

about the glove... about the man selling it. "Timothy, let's leave." She tugged on his sleeve. "Right now!" Normally, Tim would have walked away and asked questions later. But this time he couldn't. Lonegan's glove had that kind of pull.

"Go ahead," prompted the vendor, "try her on."

So Tim did, sliding his fingers into five of the six slots. The leather softened, instantly conforming to his hand. Tim wouldn't have been able to tell you how, because at first glance, the glove looked to be about double his size; and yet there it was, *the* perfect fit. But what happened next had to be the freakiest moment of all. Tim could've sworn he felt a sixth finger sprouting from his hand.

"It seems to like you," said the vendor. He cupped both hands round his mouth. "Plaaaay ball!" Tim mimed making a play in the field and could almost hear the roar of the crowd.

"How much you want for 'er?"

Willa stepped between them, keeping her back to the vendor. "We have to go, Timothy."

"Maybe *you* have to go!" he said in a surly voice that wasn't his own. Willa's legs turned to jelly. You know that shiver she felt before? Nothing compared to this one. It was as obvious as tooth decay: Tim had decided the glove was his. That made what he did next even stranger.

"I'll ask you one last time!" he barked. "How much to take this hunk of junk off your wrinkled old hands?"

Willa couldn't believe what she was hearing. Tim could be many things – awkward, lazy, occasionally silly – but rude never made the line-up.

The vendor responded, "I couldn't possibly let her go for less than... fifty dollars."

"Fifty," repeated Tim. "Fifty." And then he did something that took Willa's breath away, and not in a good way. He plucked a five-dollar note from his pocket, crumpled it into a ball and threw it at the vendor's feet. "That's all you get!" he said in that same surly voice. "And you're lucky to get that. Because if I made a run for it, you'd never catch me. Not in a million years." And with that, Tim walked away, claiming the glove as his own.

Willa was mortified. Sure, bargaining was all part of the game. It was what you did at flea markets and yard sales. But this was different; *Tim* was different. And what concerned Willa most, more than the intense voice, was the look in his eyes. She'd never seen it before.

Tim's eyes had looked... *cruel.*

She dug into her bag, taking out all the money she had,

which was about twenty dollars shy. "I'll come back tomorrow with the rest," she told the vendor.

The old man gently pushed her hand away. "Don't concern yourself, young miss," he said in a tone that suggested she should. "The boy got what he bargained for." The vendor looked relieved, like a thousand-pound tombstone had just been lifted from his chest.

By that point, Tim was almost through the exit. Willa caught him by his sleeve. "Wait up!" He turned halfway and she punched his shoulder. Hard. "What was that all about?" She was hoping the real Tim would respond.

"A total rip-off," he said with a snarky laugh.

"I agree, fifty bucks was way too much, but you didn't have to— "

"Fifty? Little girl, you are as dumb as a rock. This glove's worth ten times that amount."

"'Little girl'?" Willa cocked her fist. "Before you die, explain!"

"You wouldn't understand."

Willa placed the un-fisted hand on her hip. "Don't even."

"It's Lonegan's glove." He showed her the mitt – the thirteen, the snake tattoo. Willa was loath to admit it, but Tim was right. She didn't understand. "The dude was practically a legend," he added.

"I practically couldn't care less. What you did back there was wrong."

Tim continued, unabated. "Check it out! A six-fingered mitt wasn't patented until the nineteen sixties."

"So?"

"So!" He had to catch his breath. "This glove was specially designed for Lefty in the fifties because..." he could barely contain himself, "... Lefty Lonegan had six fingers!"

That did it. Willa was officially weirded out. Not by Lefty's unusual anatomy; her uncle Josh had three nostrils. It was Tim's delivery. The authority in his voice. As if he'd actually been there back in the day.

"Take it off!" Willa tugged at the mitt and Tim's entire body came along with it.

"Stop!" he pleaded. "You're pulling my arm out of the socket!" The glove wouldn't budge, like it was surgically grafted to Tim's wrist. Willa didn't let up. She couldn't let up! It had to come off, though she couldn't have told you why. It was that feeling in her gut. Somehow Willa knew... the glove *wasn't right*. She planted her feet, tugging with every ounce of strength she had, and for a brief moment, Willa wasn't feeling leather. She felt blood flowing through the icy veins of an enlarged hand, like it was actual skin she was touching, cold and clammy. The flesh of a dead man!

Tim saw the look on her face and then he was scared, too. "Get it off! Please, Willa, please!"

"I'm trying!"

As they pulled in opposite directions, a thought went swirling through Tim's mind: he shouldn't have ripped off the old man. It was a despicable thing to do. And with regret came release, as if the glove no longer had any use for him.

It slid into Willa's hands and she fell backwards, landing on her butt. Tim hurried to her side. "You okay, Will?" She thought about responding with a punch until she realised… the voice, it belonged to Tim. *Her* Tim. He was back.

"Get rid of it, Tim-bo."

As he helped her to her feet, Tim knew she was right. "It's going back right now." *With an apology,* he might have added, because that's exactly what he intended. But when Tim and Willa returned to where the vendor had been, the old man and the table were gone. Tim spun around in circles, hoping to find him. It was no use. It was as if the old man and the table had never been there. "Now what do I do?"

Willa softened. She assumed that they were in the wrong

spot, and she didn't want to spend the rest of her afternoon wandering around the flea market. "Enjoy your new hunk of junk," she dead-panned. Then she quickly added, "And with the money you just saved, you can buy me an ice cream. You can even tell me all about this Lefty what's-his-face."

And that's pretty much what happened. Over perfect ice creams, Tim told Willa everything he knew about Lefty Lonegan. Not just his batting average, which was a hefty .425 the year he, um, *moved on*, but also facts about his exceptional fielding skills. Lefty was being scouted by – cue the heavenly choir – the New York Yankees. That is, until that fateful night when a car crash cost him his hand. "On the day of the All-Star game, July seventeenth, nineteen fifty-five, Lefty hung himself from the centre field wall." Tim bowed his head. "Baseball was his life. Without his hand, he couldn't play. And without the game, he couldn't go on."

"That's the worst story ever," said Willa. But there were worse things about Lefty, things even Tim didn't know about. The stuff of true nightmares. **Steady yourself, dear reader, for what is about to happen to young Timothy is the stuff of true nightmares. Perhaps even yours...**

That night, when Tim took the glove home, he didn't

say a word to his parents, which was unlike him. He went to bed early, hoping he could sleep off the bizarre events of the day.

But he couldn't.

At first he blamed his sleeplessness on the heat. It was a muggy night and the ceiling fan just wasn't cutting it. Tim flipped over his pillow to find a cold spot. And from his side, he caught sight of Lonegan's glove. It was on the dresser next to his aquarium. In the dark, it looked like an overgrown human heart. Of course, it wasn't long before Tim's imagination went into extra innings and the giant heart started to beat.

*Thump... thump. Thump... thump.*

Tim did what most brave souls do when confronted with such dilemmas. He pulled the covers over his head and hoped it would stop. But the thumping continued, growing stronger. *Thump... THUMP. Thump... THUMP!*

Tim lowered the sheet, just a smidge. *Thump... THUMP. Thump... THUMP!* The sound was still with him. Increasing. *THUMP... THUMP!* It was maddening. *THUMP... THUMP!* But it wasn't the glove. Tim's eyes darted across the room and focused on a small white circle rising and falling in quick succession against the night-time sky. *THUMP... THUMP!* The sound was coming from Tim's window. And then he saw it...

A baseball was being thrown against the glass – faster than any other baseball has ever been thrown. Supernaturally fast. *THUMP... THUMP!* It was only a matter of seconds before—

*THUMP*-CRACK! The ball cracked the windowpane, splintering the glass in the shape of a spiderweb.

In one of those silly moves somebody makes in every horror movie ever made, Tim climbed out of bed to investigate. You know, to check it out. **A most excellent choice, Master Timothy. What could possibly go wrong?**

*"Yee–ouch!"* Almost instantly, a stinging pain shot through his foot. Tim looked down. Horror of horrors! He had stepped on... his social studies folder. Then he heard it again: *THUMP-CRACK!* Hopping on one foot, he made it to the window. Crouching below the sill, he looked out into the garden. And that's when it happened: *THUMP-CRASH-SMASH!* The ball blasted through the splintered pane. Tim ducked out of the way and the ball silently rolled to a stop by his foot. He instinctively reached down to grab it. The ball was caked in mud and patches of what appeared to be green mould and moss. Still, he had to pick it up. Wouldn't you?

# CHAPTER TWO

He rubbed the muck onto his pyjama sleeve so he could make out a signature – not that he needed to. He had already guessed to whom it had belonged. And as much as he hoped otherwise, the ball was indeed signed... *Lefty*.

No surprise, right? But what Tim saw next certainly was.

Gazing through the splintered glass, he spotted a figure swaying, dangling from the highest branch of an old oak tree. At first it looked like a mannequin wearing an outdated baseball uniform. Its clothes were dripping with fresh mud, like it had just slid into home or crawled out of a grave. There was a noose round its neck, and if that wasn't enough, there was a stump where the left hand should have been.

Tim froze in place. That's rule number one: when something scares you witless, you freeze. That was unfortunate, because had he been able to move, he would have noticed his fish flittering around the aquarium. Because they were scared, too. And when fish get scared, they don't freeze. They flitter.

The thumping returned. Now it was Tim doing the work, for that was the sound of his own heart pounding from his chest. He had a sneaking suspicion that he wasn't alone, like something *else* was there in the room.

He was right.

There was, in fact, something hideous on the floor. A human hand, lopped off at the wrist, hiding in plain sight. It was perfectly still, like a clay sculpture, with stalks of decaying bone protruding from its fleshy core. How had it got there? Had it come through the window with the ball? Had it been hiding inside the glove the whole time? Tim's most rational thought was that it wasn't *really* there at all. He must be dreaming. It was simply a nocturnal manifestation of the day's events. He would wake himself up and everything would be fine. So Tim closed his eyes and silently counted to three. And when he opened his eyes...

... the hand was gone. Just like that.

Tim sighed. He almost laughed, except his heart was still racing, that creeped-out feeling still with him, and with good reason. There *was* something else in the bedroom with him. He could hear it, even over the thumping of his own heart. It sounded like fingernails.

Scratching.

Tim looked around until he spotted it... *there!* A shape skittered across the floor. In the dark, you'd have sworn it was a giant spider, as big as a man's hand. Only, this spider had six legs. Get the picture? It was a severed six-fingered hand, digging its razor-sharp nails into the floorboards to drag itself forwards. But where was its body? At the moment, it was out in the garden, inconveniently hanging from a tree.

The disembodied hand picked up speed, all six digits working in horrible harmony. Moving with purpose. The wretched thing had a destination in mind: it was heading towards a dresser where its terrible prize – Lonegan's glove – was waiting to reunite with the appendage that had once given it life. Its bony fingertips reached for the knobs so it could climb.

If the hand was real, Tim reasoned, he would need to get a closer look at that thing hanging out in the yard. He reached for a pair of 'vintage' binoculars on his shelf. He panned across a section of gnarled branches until...

... a corpse's face appeared in close-up. Tim could practically smell its rancid stench through the lenses. It was Lefty Lonegan's face, or what remained of it, now more bone than flesh. A thin layer of bleached-white skin had been crudely stitched in semicircles around the temples, rendering him a human baseball. The lower jaw was rattling up and down. At first Tim thought it was a reflex, for the thing hanging in the garden was clearly dead. But then he could see that its movement was deliberate. Lefty was trying to form words. Tim couldn't hear what they were, and honestly, he wasn't so sure he wanted to. The corpse struggled to raise its left arm. (More difficult than it sounds, after rigor mortis and decades spent buried underground.) The stump hovered in mid-air, pointing at Tim, as if it deemed *him* responsible for this night of horrors.

But that wasn't even the worst of Tim's problems, because by then, the disembodied hand had ascended to the top of the dresser and was sliding all six of its bony digits into the glove. A perfect fit, one might add. After all, it was custom-made for Lonegan's hand.

Tim dropped the binoculars, because that's rule number two: when you get scared, you drop things. Unaware of what was going on behind him, he backed up to the dresser, the last place he wanted to be. His hands clasped the ledge for support. And that's when he felt it: the glove was behind him. And it was moving.

Tim didn't need to look, though he did soon enough. He snatched the glove, holding it at bay like you would a disgustingly dirty nappy and hustling to the window, with plans of returning it to Lonegan's corpse.

As Tim cocked his arm to make the throw, the glove flew out of his hand, as if of its own accord. The oversized webbing attached itself to his face. He couldn't see, couldn't breathe!

The glove was on the attack, smothering him like a leathery starfish. Tim tried everything: pulling, punching, pinching! The hand had an iron grip: they didn't call Lefty 'the six-fingered phenom' for nothing. Tim freed up his mouth long enough to manage a muffled cry for help, though it didn't carry very far. Maybe the fish heard it. But honestly, what could they do?

He had to work out a way to alert his parents before he lost consciousness. As he felt around, his fingers found his iPhone. Tim blasted the first song on his favourites list. It wasn't enough to scare off the glove, but it did bring Mum and Dad charging into the bedroom.

One of them flipped on the light. It *had* to be Tim's mum: his dad's major goal in life was turning *off* every light he ever came across.

They found Tim rolling on the floor, wrestling an empty glove. His dad pried it from his face. Tim looked up to see his parents standing over him, speechless. The mitt was once again a lifeless glob of brown leather. Yes, this required some explaining. Tim told them about the thing inside the glove, so they checked it out, and guess what they found? Go on, you can do this.

That's right. Nothing! Zero, zilch, nada. No evidence that

a disembodied six-fingered hand had ever been there. Right away, Tim's mum felt his head for fever. "I'm not imagining things!" Tim pointed to the window. "If I was, how do you explain that?"

His parents turned. "Explain what?" Tim's mother asked. The pane was in one piece. The window wasn't broken and there were no signs of a mouldy baseball or a severed hand (though Tim's foot really had done a number on his social studies folder).

Tim began to expound on the one-handed baseball player hanging from the tree, but when his parents looked outside, all they saw was the old tyre swing swaying from a branch. His mum assured him it had been a nightmare. "You're spending too much time with Club Spooky," she said.

"The Fearsome Foursome," corrected Tim, "and this has nothing to do with them."

His dad sniffed the inside of the glove. He hadn't followed the game since he was Tim's age and couldn't recall a Lefty Lonegan.

"He played for the Red Devils. Triple-A ball, way back in the fifties. Before he, well... retired early."

"What was it? An injury?"

"You might say that."

Tim's mum shook her head. "Served him right. Baseball's just a game. Maths and English skills pay bills." She kissed Tim goodnight and headed off to her bedroom. His dad stayed behind, holding the glove a moment longer. Another whiff. "Is it valuable?"

Tim shrugged. "Could be. I paid five bucks for it."

"See if you can sell it. Turn a profit. Say... six dollars. One for each finger." His dad thought that was hilarious, adding his own laugh track as he turned out the lights. "Pleasant dreams, champ." But Tim didn't laugh. And he didn't sleep. Not until the next day... during English and maths.

Later that afternoon, Tim planned on sleeping through baseball, as well. He might have taken a nap on the bench, where he spent most games, had Arty Caruthers not sprained his ankle kicking sand in some kid's face. So what was Coach Anderson to do? Forfeit the game? Or send Tim to centre field, where he could do minimal damage?

His being in the starting line-up was a happy accident. But when Tim reached into his bag, he inadvertently grabbed the wrong mitt. That's right – Lonegan's glove.

He would have switched it, except that Coach Anderson was already yelling: "Get into centre, Tom... Ted... Tim!" Tim jogged onto the field, which he could do in a relatively player-like manner. His hope was that he wouldn't embarrass himself, and for the first four batters, he didn't get the chance. There was a walk, a strikeout on three pitches, a pop-up to the catcher, and another strikeout on five. Tim was almost through the inning unscathed when Lena Toots stepped up to the plate. Lena was a big girl, and not just twelve-year-old Little League big. We're talking thirty-eight-year-old truck driver big. She took a practice swing and the pitcher winced. Tim was playing shallow and the coach waved to him, calling, "Back! Back! Back!"

Tim was still backing up when the umpire shouted, "Ball's in!"

The pitcher kicked up his left leg to begin his wind-up, then fired a fastball straight down main street… which Lena proceeded to eat like it was her third doughnut. The clang of her aluminium bat echoed into the next field, and a fly ball went soaring two hundred feet into the sky, then made its descent towards centre. Tim's teammates watched, hoping for a miracle, because that's what you did when you watched Tim cover the field. But Lonegan's glove had *other* plans.

Tim felt the sixth finger take root inside the mitt as the surly voice in his head instructed his legs to move, which they did. He got a perfect view of the ball as it travelled towards the wall. Louis Crump, playing in right, ran at it, too. He'd been instructed to make any and all plays that came Tim's way. But this was Tim's moment. Tim's and Lefty's.

The ball started to drop when, out of nowhere, Crump flew in, shouting, "I got it, loser!" Tim lowered his hands, as if giving Crump room to snag it. But as the right fielder came under the ball, Tim stuck out his foot and swept his legs. Crump went down, continuously tripping over his own two feet — one of those trips you can watch for about five minutes, wondering if the guy is ever going to land. Well, Crump landed. It looked like an accident, even to those who saw it: the ball going one way, Crump the other.

Tim ran for the wall, watching with unnatural clarity as the ball spiralled over his shoulder. He felt lighter than air now. Coming into range, he lifted his feet, climbed the wall like an insect and made the catch. There was a gasp from the stands but the play wasn't over. Tim did a complete flip, like something you'd see in the Olympics, landing on two feet and, in the same motion, firing a rocket to home.

By then, the runner on third had already tagged up. It should have been a close play, but Tim's throw missed the cut-off man. It missed because Tim bypassed the cut-off man on purpose, sending the ball home on a fly. The catcher didn't even have to move. The ball landed in the pocket of the glove like it had been born there. He dropped his arm and tagged the runner as he slid into home, a double play!

Tim's teammates went nuts. Even Crump, flat on his back, had to admit it was a spectacular play. For the record, he never called Tim 'loser' again.

As Tim trotted in from centre, his team was waiting on the field to greet him. He'd never felt that way before. Sure, Tim had aced tests; he'd even come third in the potato sack race on Sports Day. But this was different. This was baseball, the sport he so adored but had never excelled at.

This was power.

# Chapter Three

**T**im made three more plays that day, none as spectacular as the first, but all pretty nifty, especially for him. He shined at the plate, too, hitting a double and a triple and driving in four runs. That Monday, it was considered a fluke. On Wednesday, the fluke continued when Tim hit a three-run shot to win in a walk-off. By Friday, Tim had infiltrated the starting line-up. The following week, he batted lead-off. And the week after that, Coach Anderson moved him into the clean-up spot, batting fourth. It was some sort of miracle, a gift from the baseball gods.

Or was it a curse?

# THE FEARSOME FOURSOME

You see, Tim's new-found skills came with a price, and an ugly one at that. His very nature had changed. He would now do anything to ensure a win: lie, cheat, brawl. Sling insults at the other team. Insult his own teammates, like he was better than them all. Like he really was Lefty Lonegan back in the day.

And what was the benefit of all this ugliness? Oh, just that for the first time ever, Tim made the All-Star team. So typical, right? Don't go tearing your eyes out of their sockets. He'll get his.

Sometimes it takes someone on the outside to truly see what's happening. Tim couldn't see it. He had become intoxicated by his unnatural success. It was up to a friend, a real friend like Willa, to turn things around. She arrived at his house early on a Sunday with some important information, the kind that could save a soul. She found Tim in his room, staring out into the garden where the tyre swing swayed back and forth, back and forth. He was wearing Lonegan's glove.

"Timothy?" He barely looked up. Didn't even notice that she was wearing make-up, that she looked pretty. All he could manage was "What's with the skirt?"

"It was in my wardrobe."

"You can borrow some tracksuit bottoms." He stood up to

grab a pair from his drawer. "After today's game, you can sell 'em online."

"Online's for posers," said Willa. "Isn't that what you always say? A real collector needs to handle the merchandise." She knew the old Tim was in there somewhere and she was trying to draw him out. "I came to ask you not to play today."

He looked her way and laughed. "Are you nuts? It's the All-Star game. I'm an All-Star. I, Tim Maitland, made the team."

"No, Tim-bo. Lefty Lonegan made the team. It's the glove. *His* glove. There's something wrong with it."

"Guess you haven't seen me on the field."

Willa's fists tightened. "Oh, I've seen you on the field. And I've seen you off the field. You're not you any more."

"That's right. The old me got permanently benched. The new me is a superstar!"

"No! The *old* Tim was the superstar. The one who was awkward and kind and funny." Boy, she really was sounding like a girl. "The new Tim's a jerk. Everybody thinks so."

"Really? Wait till today, when you hear my cheering section."

Willa lowered her head. "I won't, Tim-bo. I won't hear anything."

"Why not?"

"Because I'm not going to the game."

"But... you gotta come, Will. It's the All-Stars."

For an instant, she heard the real Tim. The familiar sweetness in his voice. And she made the mistake a lot of strong girls make. Willa melted. "Okay, Tim-bo, I'll be there. On one condition."

"Name it."

"You have to use your own glove."

"This *is* my own glove."

"No!" Willa caught herself, not wanting to shout. "I mean your old one. The one I bought you. Think you can do that? Think you have the guts?"

Tim charged her like an angry gust of wind, backing Willa into a corner. With Tim wearing boots, they were the same height. "I got all the guts I need, doll face. Why don't you scram? Sew something. Make the beds, wash the dishes!"

Willa knew she'd better leave. If she stayed, Tim might be attending the All-Star game in traction. She started for the door, pausing when she remembered why she came. "I found this online," she said as she yanked an article from her bag. "It was buried pretty deep. But I went back years until I found it."

"What's it about?"

"Lefty Lonegan. The *real* Lefty Lonegan."

"I've forgotten more about Lefty than you'll ever know!"

"Oh, yeah? So then you knew he was into voodoo?"

Tim seemed to shrink before her eyes. Sure, he'd heard the rumours: that Lefty's skills were unnatural. But voodoo? Willa continued, "The tattoo on the mitt. The snake. The symbol. I looked it up."

"A lot of people have weird tats, Will."

"Let me finish." She was determined to get through to him: she was a girl on a mission. "It says Lefty made a deal with Houngan Atencio. He was a powerful voodoo priest who lived on the bayou. Atencio agreed to make Lefty a star, a six-fingered wonder, in exchange for ten per cent of everything he earned. At first, Lefty kept his side of the bargain. And Atencio kept his. But as his star continued to shine, Lefty conveniently forgot about the magic. He actually believed it all had to do with him. Sound familiar? By the time those major league scouts started wooing him, Lefty had stopped paying Atencio. So the voodoo priest showed up at one of his games to remind him. Lefty had him ejected from the park, humiliated, a laughing stock. And that's when Atencio cursed him… by cursing the glove."

She held up the article for Tim to see. Next to a picture of Lefty was a pencil sketch of Houngan Atencio. It was the vendor from the flea market, the old man who had sold Tim the glove.

Tim cradled the glove against his chest. "If you're trying to scare me, save it for the Fearsome Foursome."

"You don't get it, do you? It's a test!" Willa might have been guessing, but that was okay: her guesses were usually right over the plate. "What Lefty did cost him more than his hand. It cost him his soul. That's not the game, Tim-bo. That's not baseball."

"And what do you want me to do about it?" he questioned with a voice that sounded like the real Tim.

Willa sighed with relief. "Get rid of it, for a start. Bring it back to Amicus Field and bury it with Lefty. I'll help you. We'll bury it together!"

Willa looked into Tim's eyes, hoping she'd see the soul of the boy she cared for. But the thing she saw didn't have a soul. Lefty's spirit now manifested itself when Tim wasn't wearing that accursed glove. Tim's mouth had twisted into the smarmy smirk of a dirty ball player. It was Lefty's mouth. And it had a few choice words for Willa, some of which are not suitable for printing. "Get rid of it? Bury it? You want me to throw it out? I'd just as soon throw you out! How'd that be, little girl? How'd it be if I stuck you in the bin and rolled you out to the kerb?"

Willa would never have believed it before, but Tim was scaring her. And he knew it. He knew she was afraid, and it pleased him. "Gotta go, doll face." He slung his equipment bag over his shoulder. "See ya at Cooperstown." Tim blew past her, out the door and out of her life. He had an All-Star game to attend.

The game was scheduled to begin at one o'clock at Bulldog Park. Families arrived from all over town. There were ice cream vans and hot dog stands, and the deputy mayor was even there to throw out the ceremonial first pitch.

Tim watched from the dugout, losing his patience with the pre-game festivities. How many people could they possibly thank? As Lonegan's glove tightened round his wrist and a sixth digit rooted into place, he shouted from the bench: "Let's play some ball already!"

The umpire shot him a look. "You're an All-Star. Try to act like one." Tim grumbled under his breath. The umpire approached. "What was that?"

"Nothing, blue. Just clearing my throat." The umpire locked eyes with Tim. "Next time you're out of here." The glove caused a tickle in Tim's hand. It was trying to get him to laugh at the silly little man in the umpire's uniform. Tim bit down on his lip, fighting the urge, waiting for the umpire to walk away.

Coach Anderson leant in. "What's the matter with you?"

"Nothin', Coach. I'm a hundred and fifty per cent."

"There's no such thing as a hundred and fifty per cent. Clean up your act before you get sent off."

"Sure thing, Coach. Whatever you say."

After the school marching band massacred 'The Star-Spangled Banner', it was time to play ball. Tim's team took to the field. He was starting at first, not his usual position, but unusual things happened at All-Star games. Just ask Lefty.

Right away, a kid looped one over the shortstop's head, dropping it in for a hit. Tim was sure to let the batter know when he reached first that it was a lucky shot. Lonegan's voice whispered in Tim's ear: *Tell him his grandma hits better than that.* So Tim told him.

The pitcher made a pick-off attempt, throwing the ball to first. Tim swung his arm to make the tag, smacking the kid harder than he had to, shoving him off the base and tagging him out. It was a cheap move, one not befitting an All-Star.

But perfectly legal. As Lefty used to say back in the day, "All's fair in love and war and baseball."

The crowd jeered and Tim laughed. He laughed like a hyena. Like Lefty Lonegan.

In fact, he laughed his way through three complete innings. And when he wasn't laughing, he was shooting rays of sunlight into the eyes of the opposing outfielders with his mirrored sunglasses. A fine day at the ballpark. Rah-rah-rah, Master Lefty. Oh, I'm sorry. I meant, Master Timothy.

It was the bottom of the fourth inning when Tim entered the batter's box for his second, and final, go at bat. On the first pitch, he took a wild swing and the bat flew from his hands, helicoptering all the way to the mound, where it almost nailed the pitcher in the shins. Hey, bats slip. It happens. You can't prove anything. But if you check the record books, you'll see Lefty Lonegan did the same thing back in the day.

The umpire had seen enough and, as threatened, ejected Tim from the game. That was just as well: Coach Anderson was about to do the same.

Tim grabbed Lonegan's glove, his only friend, from the bench and walked across the field to a chorus of hisses. And he continued walking for what seemed like miles before starting to run. It wasn't an especially graceful run, but that was a good thing. It meant he was running like Tim. And all the while he was thinking about the crummy things he'd done. About the mess he'd made with Willa. She was right, of course. It was the glove, not him. The glove was evil.

When Tim finally slowed down to get his bearings, he found himself in the centre of a car park. But there were no cars, only weeds sprouting from every unpaved crevice. Where was he? Tim shuddered when he worked it out. It was the flea market where he'd first laid eyes on the accursed glove.

He passed through the front gate, and when he came out on the other side, Tim found himself standing on a ball field. He located the scoreboard over the right field wall. He could make out some lettering, faded from the sun. No, it couldn't be. It wasn't possible. The date said July 17, 1955. Tim's heart skipped two beats. It was the day of the All-Star game, the one Lefty never got to play, although he did make a swinging appearance out in the field.

The sound of an organ crackled from the stadium's tinny loudspeakers. *Da – da – da – da – da – daaaaaah!* "Charge!" yelled the organist. Tim could see him from the field. It was good ole Rusty McCallum, dead twenty years.

What was left of him was back in the booth. Those bones played a mean pipe organ.

Now the crowd was arriving. Hordes of corpses settled into the seats with their balloons and their banners held up high, a nightmare in the daytime.

It was time for a quick getaway! Tim made a move for the exit but the players were already taking to the field, blocking his escape. There were eight figures in various uniforms, All-Stars in their time. Today you could scarcely call them human. They were more like living skeletons, in differing stages of putrefaction. Some of them were legless, crawling out of the dugout like slugs. Others were exposing their crumbling rib cages, airing out their rotted entrails.

Tim tried to appeal to their, uh… better natures. "You got it all wrong. I don't belong here! I'm not even a real All-Star!" But the shuffling piles of decayed flesh cared little about what he had to say. They simply kept on coming, forcing Tim back onto the first-base line. There was no escape. Nowhere for him to run. He was part of the team now. And his time had come to…

"Plaaaaay ball!" called out a thing from behind the catcher. It was the umpire. A description of how it looked would cause you to skip dessert for a year.

The lead-off batter, a one-handed collection of bones in a tattered Devil Rays uniform, stepped up to the plate. Number thirteen. Lefty. He was holding a Louisville Slugger in his right hand, not coincidentally, the only hand he had. He pointed the fat end at Tim, who somehow found himself covering first. Strange things happen all the time at All-Star games. Especially ones being played by the dead.

"I want my glove baaaaaaack," Lefty gurgled in a voice that belonged to the grave. Perhaps it was that unfortunate incident with the noose, but his elocution was plain awful.

Tim yanked the glove as hard as he could, but like a newly grafted appendage, it wouldn't come off. So he pulled at it some more, screaming with each yank, over and over again, but to no avail. "It doesn't come off!" he tried explaining. If only Lefty had had ears.

The putrid vision on the pitcher's mound – a right-hander might be the polite way to describe it – sent a sinker over the plate. Lefty was all over it like rot on a zombie, connecting with a one-armed swing. A dribbler moved up the first-base line, an easy play. But Tim was too busy wrestling with the glove to notice. The ball passed straight through his legs and entered the outfield.

The crowd went wild, *clackety-clack* clapping with their

bony digits, but an error was the least of Tim's problems. Lefty was now chugging towards first base. "I want my glove baaaaaack." The undead thing was coming for him, as unstoppable as the game itself. Again, Tim tried explaining: "It won't come off!" But Lefty wasn't buying any excuses. He had a thick skull. Literally.

Tim abandoned first base before Lefty crossed the bag. "I want my glove baaaaaack." Tim rounded second, then third, on his way to home base. His plan was to keep on going, straight through to the exit. But he broke the first rule of base running. He turned and looked. One tiny mistake and it cost him. Tim tripped, falling forwards, his arms sticking straight out to protect him from the fall. He hit the ground in a face-first slide and, through it all, retained the overwhelming desire to complete the play.

As luck would have it, the ball arrived from the cut-off man – make that the cut-off *thing* – about the same time Lefty ambled towards home base. "I want my glove baaaaaaack!"

Tim scooped the ball out of the dirt and, as he pivoted to make the tag, yelled into the hole that had once been Lefty's ear: "So take it!"

Did Tim make the play? Was Lefty safe? Or was he dead on arrival?

They're still debating it in the netherworld. There was no instant replay. And the umpire behind home plate no longer had his eyes. But Lefty did take back what was his – over that there is no dispute. The crowd of living corpses settled into a respectful silence as they listened to the exquisite popping sounds emanating from the field: bones being separated from bones as limbs were relieved of their sockets. Talk about a seventh-inning stretch. Lefty dismantled Tim, piece by piece, until all that remained in the centre of home plate was Lonegan's glove.

Tim's disembodied head rolled to the pitcher's mound, arguing the play as it went. "You were out! Out by a million miles!"

"Safe," insisted Lefty as he staggered towards the pitcher's mound. Tim had done wrong by the game. And now the game had done wrong by him. His head watched from the mound as number thirteen retrieved his glove and reattached it to his rotting stump. Lefty sauntered off across the field, his skeletal form slowly disappearing into the shimmering glow of the stadium lights.

# Chapter Four

The librarian completed the final passage and looked up from the page. "Lefty certainly got a piece of that one. What do they call that in baseball? A singleheader?"

The others remained dumbfounded. Not even a groan. Steve was the first to comment. "Lame, lame, lame. Why in the world would Lefty come back as a zombie?"

The floor was now open – that's how the Fearsome Foursome's meetings worked – so Willa chimed in with an opinion. "That *was* a little weak."

"Pray tell, elaborate."

"Well, for starters, having Tim rip off the old man makes him an unsympathetic lead."

The librarian nodded. "An excellent observation." He looked at Tim. "Would you not agree?"

But Tim didn't answer. He didn't move. He just stood there, white as a sheet. Noah weighed in with his thoughts, too. "Not to be rude, but that whole voodoo angle? They did it a hundred times in the old horror comics."

The librarian had a blank expression on his face. "Horror... comics?"

"Dude, it's the twenty-first century. Make it an Internet curse."

Steve shook his head. "Naaaah." As usual, he had a critique for the critique. "The Internet's so been there, done that. And don't get me started on that whole baseball plot line."

The librarian appeared flabbergasted. "It is no longer the national pastime?"

"Sure. And that's the problem. You have to think globally. I would have gone with soccer. It's got worldwide marketability."

The librarian lowered his head in a respectful bow. "Impressive. You three certainly know your genre. Of course, we have not heard from the lead, as the young lady so aptly referred to... Master Timothy himself."

# CHAPTER FOUR

The three friends turned to look. Tim hadn't moved, except for his left arm, which was now raised above his lap. "I picked it up at a flea market," he whispered mournfully. He was wearing Lonegan's glove.

The others appeared startled, but the librarian's morbid appetite had been satisfied. "The genuine article, is it not? May I see?"

Tim shook his head. "It... it won't come off."

The remark sent shivers throughout the group and, remember, shivers were their speciality. By then, Noah was seeing things Steve's way: it was time to adios. Yet there were no visible entrances, which also meant no visible exits. He started checking bookshelves, hoping to find a trip switch or a lever. "There's got to be a secret passage."

"Oh, yes," confirmed the librarian, "the house is filled with secrets." That sent more chills up and down their spines as it became obvious: the librarian had no intention of allowing them to leave. At least, not yet.

Steve cut to the chase. "Okay, old man. I'll play your game. Read mine next!"

The librarian's smile expanded as wide as a jack-o'-lantern's. "So eager, are we? *Daring* me to get yours over with?"

"Wh-why'd you say that?"

The librarian had hit a nerve, not just for Steve, but for the others as well. "I think we'll save yours for last."

Steve plopped down into an antique chair, where he remained in obedient silence, awaiting the next tale. For the others, *that* was scary! They'd never seen him back away from a challenge before. Then again, Steve had never been challenged by the likes of the librarian before.

The talking skull – ahem, librarian – turned his attention to Willa. "The young lady has something she needs to hear. Isn't that right, Mistress Willa?" Yes, he knew her name, and no, she didn't ask how. They had already gone through that routine with Tim.

Willa moved in close, like it was part of the rules – rules she somehow seemed to understand.

The librarian held out the book, gesturing for her to turn to the next chapter. So she did, her bracelet sounding like a wind chime as she flipped the page. The librarian's finger touched the charms as he identified the animals. "The rabbit. The parrot. The goldfish." He stopped short of naming the fourth charm, for that was Willa's job.

"The guinea pig," she said, tears welling from her eyes.

The librarian glanced down at the book. The next chapter had arrived. Willa's story. So he began to read...

# Chapter Five

## WITCH-BONE

# Pets live. They eat. They poop. They die.

It's what they do.

Chubs died peacefully in the night. One hopes. There were no witnesses. But Willa's guinea pig certainly wasn't playing dead when she found him keeled over in his cage. He'd gone the way of her goldfish, her parrot and her rabbit. More or less.

Pets die. It's what they do.

Willa's family gathered that same morning to bury Chubs in the garden. There was a modest pet cemetery a few feet from Mum's veggie garden, with markers for the beloved creatures that had come and gone before him.

A cardboard casket containing Chubs's remains was lowered into a hole, twelve inches deep. The box used to contain frozen strawberry strudels until about a half hour before, when Billy ate the last one. Willa's dad asked her if she would care to say a few words. She was trying to keep her emotions in check. All Willa could manage was, "I love you, Chubs." She sprinkled dirt onto the carton.

"Mmm. Strawberries. The best he ever smelt," were the only words of comfort Willa would be receiving from that little brat she called a brother. Billy was two years younger. And even though Willa didn't have a complete memory of the world before him, she was fairly convinced they were the happiest two years of her life.

"Billy!" chastised their mum. "Show a little respect." Dad just shook his head. That's all you could do with Billy.

But Billy didn't apologise. That wasn't his way. Billy never said he was sorry for anything. And the funny part was Chubs had been his pet to begin with. He'd arrived one Christmas, wrapped in a bow.

In the beginning, Billy took good care of Chubs; the best he could, Willa supposed. He even picked out the stupid name, on account of Chubs's obvious weight issue. But by the time January rolled around, the writing was on the wall.

Billy was incapable of taking care of a pet. The cage was never cleaned, the water rarely replaced. And that was when Willa inherited Chubs for good. He moved into her room and had lived there ever since. Until that morning.

Now he lived in a frozen strudel box.

Willa knew the rest of the routine all too well. In about an hour, her father would ask, "Do you want another one?" as if Chubs was as replaceable as an ice cream cone.

After the funeral, Willa moped back to her room and plopped down on her bed. She wished she could sleep forever. Or at least until Friday. There was a soft knock at her door. Willa's head shot up. *Please,* she thought, *anyone but Billy.* Then she realised it couldn't be him. The knock was way too polite.

Willa's mum entered, carrying a tray with tea and fresh apricot scones. It was time for the talk. The 'pets eat, they poop, they die' speech. Willa could practically recite it in her sleep. After a bite of a scone, she said, "I don't want to talk about it."

To Willa's surprise, neither did her mum. She had come with a gift. "Put out your wrist." Willa did so and her mum slipped on a new bracelet – its four charms representing her deceased pets. "I just heard the weather report," her mum continued, changing the subject. "It's going to be a beautiful night. Why not have a few friends over for a sleepover? Dad could pitch a tent in the garden."

To Willa, this seemed like a terrible idea. The last thing she felt like doing was hearing Kayla, Tanisha and Cassidy babble on about boys and pedicures while Chubs lay rotting under the earth. Maybe if Tim was allowed to attend… but sleepovers had a strict no-boys policy. And besides, Tim had a big game the next day.

Her mum wouldn't let up. "You can make s'mores. Tell a few ghost stories. Good times for all."

*Hmm.* Sounding better. A tent in the garden was always spooky fun. Maybe a sleepover would help her forget, if just for a little while. Willa always loved a good s'more. But not as much as she loved a good ghost story.

It was just after midnight. The girls were huddled together in the centre of the tent, Cassidy at maximum-level annoying. Too much sugar or hormones or both. She was grilling Willa about Steve's 'availability', to which Willa replied, "We're twelve. We're all available." But the endless gossip did take Willa's mind off Chubs… temporarily.

# CHAPTER FIVE

Now don't go swallowing your tongue just yet. Young Willa will be thinking about her dearly departed pet soon enough. Oh, they all will.

The breeze picked up and soon the tent was rattling like mad. So much for the weather report. Willa went outside to reinforce the stakes. Tanisha was already suggesting they pack it in. But that wasn't happening. Mother Nature was letting them know the time was right for the next phase of the sleepover. The final phase. And there would be very little sleeping after that.

After returning to the tent, Willa adjusted the light on a retrofitted lantern. The mood was just right. "Kayla. Why don't you show Cass and Tanny what you brought?" Willa already knew what was in the tiny felt pouch. It was something new and ought to be good for a few giggles.

Kayla held up the pouch, announcing its contents. "Behold... an actual witch-bone!"

Tanisha wrinkled her nose. "A witch-bone? What's a witch-bone?" Now *that* was a mystery.

Kayla slipped two fingers into the pouch. "The gypsy lady said it has great power." She did her best gypsy lady voice. "But von must use de caution ven von vishes ta invok de undervorld."

The others looked at her cockeyed before issuing a collective "WHAT?"

Kayla sighed, then repeated the gypsy lady's words in her regular voice. "One must use caution when one wishes to invoke the underworld."

"OH."

Tanisha shook her head. "Those people are all fakes. My dad says that psychics and people who say they have powers aren't real, otherwise they'd be rich. They'd know all the lottery numbers the day before and they'd win a million dollars every time. Was the gypsy lady rich?"

Cassidy tilted her head. "Uh-duh! She worked in a carnival."

"That's what I thought."

It would be about two seconds before they were talking boys again. Willa needed to reel them back in. She held the lantern under her chin, giving her face an unworldly glow. "The spirit world has no use for money. They only want your soul!" With her best creepy cackle, Willa turned off the lantern. *Click!* Pitch-black.

She was hoping for screams.

Nothing came. She waited. Talk about a non-reaction. They didn't even beg for the light to come back on – though they were thinking it. The wind was really doing a number on the tent. Finally, Tanisha broke down. "Lights, please!"

Willa held out a few more seconds; then the lantern popped on and the others were looking at a face they wouldn't soon forget. Willa's eyes had turned white, her hair was sticking straight up and she was chanting in a witchy voice, "I'm gonna get you, I'm gonna get yooooou!"

The girls scrambled to the opposite side of the tent. Tanisha's lip quivered. Cassidy made a cross with two fingers. Kayla sat on a juice box. *Squirt!*

Willa couldn't hold the look any longer. Her pupils rolled down from her skull and she burst into hysterics. "Sorry, but I had to!" It was a face she'd done for the Fearsome Foursome about a billion times. Of course, it no longer had the desired effect on Tim, Noah and Steve. "Willa's doing the eye thingy again. Oh, I'm soooo scared." But on Kayla, Cassidy and Tanisha, it worked like a chilling charm.

"That wasn't funny," said Tanisha. A lull of disquiet took over the tent. Had Willa gone too far? If you were reading Happy Camp Diaries, yes, too far. Correct me if I'm wrong, but this is still Tales from the Haunted Mansion, which means Willa hadn't gone far enough.

To her relief, the silence was broken by laughter.

Apparently, Cassidy and Tanisha had just got the memo: it was fun to get scared, as long as you knew it was pretend. Like on a roller coaster. Or at a haunted house.

Yet for some reason, Kayla hadn't joined in. "Silence!" she commanded. The girls settled down. "Where was I?" It didn't sound like Kayla was asking. More like she was *telling*. She looked transformed, as if she was holding her own seance circle of sorts, and channelling someone else's spirit. Perhaps it was the gypsy lady, Madam Whoever, with instructions from the beyond.

"Proceed, Madam Kayla," said Willa, keeping with the mood.

Kayla shot her an icy look. "I am not Kayla." *Good one*, thought Willa. *She's really selling it.*

She sold it, all right. Kayla's manner was creepy and authentic. A well timed *boo* would have sent Cassidy and Tanisha skyrocketing through the roof. On any other night, Willa would have gone for it. But after the scary-eye thingy, she didn't want to risk a mass exodus. She was having too much fun for that.

Kayla removed the witch-bone from the pouch. If we're being honest, it looked exactly like a turkey wishbone dipped in varnish.

"What's it do?" asked Tanisha.

Cassidy cringed. "It looks like a regular wishbone. They come free with the bird. And just so you know, I'm going vegan, so I'm not touching it!"

Willa quickly did some damage control. "No worries. It's a witch-bone, not a wishbone. Isn't that right, Madam Whoever?" Kayla nodded.

And just like that, Cassidy was on board. "Oh, okay. As long as it's not turkey." The moment was capped off by a series of thunderclaps, loud and ominous. Suddenly, no one was laughing. Not even Willa. "Oh, man. It was supposed to be a perfect night. Maybe we should get inside."

"Amen to that!" seconded Tanisha.

"But it is. It *is* a perfect night," responded Kayla, channelling Madam Whoever.

Cassidy pointed to a tiny scroll tied to one of the bone stems. "What's that, a recipe?"

Kayla tried to remember. "She called it… intervention."

Willa suppressed a smile. "An incantation."

"How do you know?" snapped Kayla. "Were you there?"

"No. But I know about these things." Cassidy and Tanisha nodded in agreement. Willa was all about the scary. "An incantation is a spell," she continued. "When you say certain words in a certain order, they can bring about…" Willa paused for dramatic effect, "… change."

Cassidy and Tanisha were now sharing a feeling of impending doom. Or maybe it was the s'mores. Either way, it wasn't good.

"Read it," insisted Willa.

"I shouldn't. Not tonight!" Kayla protested. Tanisha and Cassidy agreed: just call it a night while they still had their lungs.

"The witch-bone demands it. You must!"

With the wind simmering down to a respectable hum, Willa raised the lantern so Kayla could read the scroll. The words were written in red ink. **Red 'ink'. Quite the coincidence, is it not, dear reader?** " 'Whoever breaks the bone you see, a single wish shall grant to thee.' "

Willa was watching for the girls' reactions. Cassidy and Tanisha were spellbound. "So what you're saying is, like, the first one to break the witch-a-majig in half gets a wish?" said Cassidy, paraphrasing what she thought she'd heard.

"That's right." Willa nodded. "The first girl to snap the witch-bone gets her wish granted."

Cassidy rubbed her hands together. "Send it on down. Tonight I'll be hanging with Steve-o."

The others got a laugh out of that. Soon there were smiles all around. The idea of having one's wishes come true always brings out a person's fun side.

**Try it, right now. Close your eyes and make a wish. But be cautious. There is a terrifying truth in the old saying, 'Be careful what you wish for'. Now read on...**

The witch-bone passed from girl to girl, each one separately sharing a favourite desire. Kayla had always wanted to see Tokyo. She twisted the bone but it would not snap. "Fail," the other girls said.

Cassidy wished her skin would clear up before her thirteenth birthday. She wrenched it the opposite way. "Another fail," Cassidy said.

Next up, Tanisha wished her father would lose thirty pounds... by morning. How'd she do? Put it this way: her dad woke up three pounds heavier. "Epic fail," the other girls yelled. They were really getting into the game now.

Last, the witch-bone found its way to Willa. The girls couldn't wait to hear what the future horror writer had to say. What would she wish for? The zombie apocalypse? A vampire's masquerade ball? Or something simpler but, to twelve-year-old girls, no less frightening: to marry Tim Maitland?

Kayla rubbed her hands together. "This is gonna be large."

Willa closed her eyes and considered the possibilities. What if something like a witch-bone really did exist? What if the wishes people made on shooting stars and birthday candles actually came to pass? There was so much to ask for. So many wonderful things to accomplish. People to save, diseases to cure. Annoying siblings to eliminate. **Now, now, Willa. Mustn't go there.**

She took her time, giving it some actual thought. As if it was reality. As if the witch-bone was real. Cassidy couldn't stand it any more. "Uh, today. While we're young!"

Willa zeroed in on a wish. The perfect choice. The only choice she could make on a day that started out as terribly as that one had. Willa opened her mouth and said the words: "I wish…"

An explosion of thunder rocked the neighbourhood, setting off car alarms and swallowing Willa's every syllable. Whatever she said couldn't be heard – not by the girls, not by Willa herself. But the witch-bone understood.

When the rumbling skies settled down, Tanisha was the first to ask: "Well? What was it?"

"What?"

"Your wish. What'd you ask for?"

Kayla threw up her hand in protest. "No... be quiet!"

This wasn't part of the routine. Everyone else had said theirs. "Why?" asked Cassidy. "What's the big deal?"

"Because." Kayla pointed to Willa's hand. "If she says it, it might not come true." What was she talking about? Willa looked down. The witch-bone had snapped in half.

Well, it didn't much matter what Kayla had to say. Cassidy and Tanisha wouldn't sleep until they knew, unloading a barrage of guesses, from the real to the ridiculous. Willa shook her head after every last one. She shook her head so many times that at one point she actually thought it might unscrew and roll off.

**Regrettably, it did not. (The disembodied head happened in the previous story.)**

After about the hundred and eleventh guess, with Willa contemplating pulling every last strand of hot-pink hair from her skull, she decided to give the girls something, anything, to shut them up. So Willa said, "World peace."

Tanisha and Cassidy glared at her like they'd been personally insulted. "World what? No way! You wasted a perfectly good wish on world peace?" This was a terrible finale for what, to them, might have included designer shoes, trips to Paris or brand-new Ferraris. World peace? *Yawn.*

Willa rolled onto her side, zipping the sleeping bag over her face. "Goodnight." The ground wasn't very comfy. Maybe she should have wished for a bed.

Within a few minutes, the girls were conked out, dreaming of designer shoes and trips to Paris in their brand-new Ferraris. Well, except for Willa, that is.

Willa crept into the garden, past the vegetable patch, to the muddy rectangle where the family pets had been interred. Where Chubs had been laid to rest that very morning. The ground between her pink toenails was still moist. And twelve inches below, a furry carcass that used to be Chubs began stirring inside its cardboard casket. The eyes bolted open, and before it even knew where it was, the undead guinea pig began gnawing its way out of its plastic zipper sandwich bag. Next there was the cardboard casket, which was no match for the rodent's expanded fangs. The dirt would be an obstacle. It always was. But Chubs was a natural-born digger. Or a natural-dead one; take your pick. The guinea pig tunnelled its way up through the loosely packed earth, forging a path to the world of the living. Air. Freedom. Food!

Willa saw the dirt jiggle by her feet. It was him, her

Chubsy-wubsy bear. Sort of. She dropped to her knees, scooping away the top layer of dirt by hand. She would set him free. Render mouth-to-mouth if necessary.

The rounded face of her resurrected rodent jiggled its way up to the surface. It was Chubs, or what Chubs had become. Those once warm chestnut eyes were now blazing orbs of fire, matching the beast's ravenous appetite. It didn't wait for Willa, its former servant in life, to pluck its plump torso from the grave. The Chubs-thing did all the work, twisting and pulling as it extracted itself out of the ground, while Willa watched, sick with terror.

Now it was free.

Willa fell back onto her elbows, trying to distance herself. But the Chubs-thing kept coming, ambling towards her, a legion of writhing maggots hitching a ride on its dirt-covered form. Willa knew at once, as soon as it crawled up her leg and headed for her throat, that the pet she had so adored had little in common with the thing she now feared. The Chubs-thing opened its mouth wide – far too wide to be normal – and unveiled its upper incisors, now longer and sharper, having been nourished by the earth just like her mum's veggies.

*Rrrrreeeeech!*

It unleashed a ghastly cry, the hunger pangs of the dead. Willa recognised its foul smell: cardboard and strawberry extract mixed with rot. The creature's intent was painfully clear – *painfully* being the operative word. It was way past dinner time, and Chubs expected to be fed.

And we all know what zombies eat!

# Chapter Six

**W**illa's eyes opened with a jolt. She found herself back in the tent, entangled in her sleeping bag. Somehow, the monstrous screech still seemed to be hanging in the air. Bad dream, right? Yeah, sure, *whatever you say.*

The other girls were still asleep, but Willa heard a ghastly sound coming from the corner of the tent. She switched on the lantern to discover… Kayla, snoring like a rhino. She really had to get that deviated septum checked out.

By then, Willa was wide awake. She thought about reading; she always brought a scary book with her. But that would only stimulate the old noggin, and then she'd be up forever. And Willa wanted to sleep. Maybe a little fresh air would do the trick. Fortunately, the weather had settled to match the earlier prediction. There was no thunder, no lightning. As her mum had said, it was a beautiful night.

So Willa did what one always does in one of these stories. She climbed out of her sleeping bag and, with the lantern as her only companion, unzipped the tent and ventured outside. Just like in her dream. Except this time, she was awake. Good move, Willa. This should work out well for you. Heh-heh-heh.

A thin layer of fog veiled the earth below her feet. Not a problem. Willa knew the route by heart. She would visit the pet cemetery, paying her respects not only to Chubs but to her rabbit, her parrot and her goldfish, the pets who were represented on her bracelet.

But as she entered the garden, something crunched under her foot. Willa didn't want to look down. Oh, but she had to. It was the frozen strudel casket, gnawed to bits. She swung the lantern round, bringing the rest of the garden into the light.

What she saw would break her mother's heart. The veggies had been ravaged! Tomatoes had been turned to ketchup. Cucumbers and lettuce… bye-bye. And the radishes, well, they were… actually, completely untouched. Apparently, the creature responsible didn't like radishes.

# CHAPTER SIX

Willa didn't know whether to return to the tent or keep on searching. She went with choice number two, because this is one of those stories and that was one of those nights. **A fiendishly good sign that things are about to get messy, which is why you came, of course.**

Willa entered the pet cemetery, kneeling by the first marker: Goldie the goldfish, the grave undisturbed. She moved on to the next: Rudy the rabbit, also intact. *Rest well, old bean.* The third, um… plot, if you will, belonged to Polly the parrot. The grave was still visible where Willa had planted the bird two and a half years before. Catching worms was no longer a problem; get the drift?

Then there was the last grave, the one she had come to see. The lantern rattled, Willa's arm shaking from nerves. It seemed she was expecting something awful, like the rest of us. And the moment did not disappoint.

Instead of finding Chubs's grave, she discovered an empty hole. Chubs, or whatever he'd become, had chewed his way out of the ground. For real.

*Crack!* A twig snapped. Isn't that always the way? Something was out there, spying on Willa from amongst the trees.

"Chubs?"

That was a funny thing to say, particularly since Chubs had never answered, even when he was alive. But it was just her way of letting him know that she was still Willa. That she meant him no harm. If only Chubs had been thinking the same. But zombie brains don't work that way. They think about food, mostly. They'll eat anyone.

*Rrrrreeeeech!*

It was that feral screech again – the one from her dream – except now she wished she was dreaming.

The hairs on Willa's neck stood on end, and no, they weren't blue, pink, purple or green. They were dirty blonde, if you must know. Dirty-blonde indicators that she was being followed.

Willa tiptoed through the ravaged garden, careful not to run. She couldn't afford to excite whatever was lurking beyond the trees... because when you run, certain animals think it's playtime. And Willa had no intention of getting playful with a zombied-out guinea pig, even one that used to be Chubs.

She made it back to the tent, climbed inside and zipped it closed. She was panting by then, expecting the worst as she steadied the lantern over the remaining sleeping bags, hoping not to find her BFFs in the same condition as her mum's veggies. But all three girls appeared unharmed, asleep as Willa had left them... until she woke two of them up.

"Guys! Guys! We have a problem!"

Cassidy's eyes opened first. She was always up for a good problem. Before she even heard what Willa had to say, she gave Tanisha a kick in the bottom. "Something's up!" Tanisha sat up, groggy, hoping it was more s'mores. All she got was a frantic rant from Willa.

"It happened! It came true! We have to get out of here! My wish came true!"

Tanisha managed to speak. "What time is it?"

"It doesn't matter! He's back. Chubs is back!"

"What are you talking about?"

"My wish. It came true. Chubs came back from the dead!"

Tanisha and Cassidy stared at her, not uttering a word. And then, having decided it was another one of Willa's patented scare routines, they both plopped onto their pillows. "Turn that light out when you're done."

Willa couldn't believe it. *No way!* How could anyone fall asleep after what she'd just told them? And what about Kayla? She never even woke up! Meanwhile, there was a thing – a grotesque, drooling, ravenous and all those other adjectives thing – just outside, searching for food.

Willa adjusted the lantern, making it daylight in the tent. Tanisha covered her eyes. "Go 'way!"

Willa didn't know what to say or do to convince them. *Rrrreeeeech!* A helping claw arrived in the form of a screech, clearly not human. Cassidy and Tanisha bolted up fast. "What was that?" Tanisha asked.

"I'm pretty sure… Chubs," Willa said softly, her eyes starting to water. And since Willa wasn't that good of an actress, Cassidy had begun to believe.

"You're serious?"

"As serious as a heart attack. Which I'm about to have. Somebody wake up Kayla."

Cassidy and Tanisha went to work on Kayla, rocking her back and forth. She was one tough specimen, could probably sleep through an earthquake. Or even the zombie-pet apocalypse. When yelling in Kayla's ear didn't work, Cassidy donated a face-full of mineral water. Kayla's right eye opened halfway. "It raining in here?"

Willa explained, "It's my fault. I wished my pets would be alive again."

Cassidy felt betrayed. "I thought you wished for world peace?"

"I did. Out loud it's what I always wish for. But in my

head I'd already made my other wish. The real wish. And I think it came true, because Chubs is back. And there's something else: I think he's hungry. He gets real mean when he's hungry!" She took a breath before adding, "He especially loves toes!"

*Phew!* The girls shared a nervous chuckle over that one. They decided Willa was just up to her usual tricks. That is, until she extended her right foot and wiggled her toes. Why hadn't they noticed before? Willa's little toe was a gnarled stub, having been chewed to the bone.

The girls shrieked and backed away from Willa like she had the plague, scrunching their toes so the ravenous Chubs-thing wouldn't get them. **And now the screaming starts! Oh, what sweet music.**

Willa didn't respond. Didn't smile. There was no laughter, no high-fiving. And this wasn't a special effect. Her little toe was, in fact, half missing for real, which explained her complete disinterest in the buy-one, get-one flip-flop sale a week earlier. *Rrrrreeeeech!* The unearthly screech returned. "It's right outside!" Kayla yelled. "What do we do?"

The undead beast was—

"There!" Tanisha pointed. The canvas fluttered behind them. The girls crawled to the centre of the tent, watching in terror as a gigantic shadow, ten times the size of the average guinea pig, circled from the garden. Someone yelled to turn out the light, and suddenly there was darkness, except for the beastly silhouette just outside the tent. Fingers pointed as the girls shrieked and the wind howled. It was pandemonium.

"It's there! Over there!"

"No! Now it's there!"

The thing was toying with them. Plotting its first meal. Now the girls were looking to Willa for solutions. It was her undead pet, after all. "What do we do?" Cassidy asked.

"Call the house!" cried Kayla.

Willa shook her head. Her dad took the phone off the hook on weekends: he liked to sleep in. "What about your brother?" suggested Cassidy.

"What's he gonna do? Annoy it to death?" Again came the terrible sound, making their skin crawl. It was horrible enough to motivate Willa to text Billy, the lesser of two evils. But before she could press send, Tanisha was pointing again. "Oh my god, look!"

The oversized shape was lurking just beyond the canvas wall, and it was suddenly making a different sound.

# CHAPTER SIX

The worst sound imaginable. The thing was digging, tunnelling a path *under* the tent wall so it could get inside.

The girls froze. Ah, scare rule number one rears its disembodied head. Willa dropped her phone. Rule number two, right on cue. Moving as a single unit, the girls shifted to the opposite side of the tent. Watching. Waiting for the ravenous thing to claw its way in so it could make a midnight snack of their pedicured tootsies.

Cassidy spoke the words the others were thinking. "Why? Why would you make such a stupid wish?"

Willa didn't have to think about that one. An answer came so fast it simply had to be the truth. "Because... I loved him," she replied. "Because I wanted another chance to say 'I love you, Chubs', instead of 'I hate you, Chubs, for biting me'..." She added softly, "Which was the last thing I ever said to him while he was alive."

Willa was sobbing. Under normal circumstances, the others might have joined in. They weren't insensitive. But they still had a giant, ravenous, undead guinea pig to deal with.

Cassidy put her arm round Willa. "I'm so sorry, sweetie. Chubs was a loyal pet." She picked up the heavy skillet they'd used to make s'mores. "But now it's time to whack him over the head!" She demonstrated her technique. "One quick whack! Get the brain, get the ghoul. And it's over." Tanisha and Kayla concurred: it was a sensible plan.

The girls formed a circle. It would be rock, paper, scissors to decide who the unlucky whacker would be. But Willa interrupted the round almost before it began. "Stop!" She took the skillet from Cassidy's hand. "It has to be me. Chubs was my responsibility. I have to do it." Now here's the thing: the others loved Willa; they cared for her like a sister. But when it came to taking on an undead critter in the middle of the night... *please allow us to unzip the tent for you on your way out.*

And that is exactly what happened. Willa took a deep breath. "I'll try to draw him out. As soon as you hear me say the coast is clear, make a run for the house." The girls nodded. Kayla unzipped the tent. Willa lifted the skillet and, with all nine and a half toes leading the charge, ventured off into the wilds of her garden.

*Zip-zap-zip!* The tent was zipped up in what had to be record time.

Willa slowly made her way round the perimeter of the tent. She didn't know what she would do if she ran into

# CHAPTER SIX

Chubs. But splattering his brains with the skillet was never really an option. Besides, she wouldn't have to. He'd still be Chubs. Larger. Hungrier. His overall demeanour much more *Night of the Living Dead*ish, but he'd still be her little Chubsy-wubsy bear. She could reason with him. Offer him a s'more. If worse came to the worst, the rest of her toe.

"How you doing out there?" whispered Kayla from inside before the others shushed her.

Willa couldn't afford to give away her position, so she said nada. She was just about there. Her heart raced as she crept round a corner of the tent to see...

... three-pronged gardening claws shoved into the dirt. It was one of her mum's tools. And next to that, Willa saw her dad's shop light propped up on the lawn, a tiny cut-out of a guinea pig taped to the bulb, making the oversized silhouette on the canvas wall.

Willa was starting to get the picture. It was a prank, of course. It had to be. A zombie guinea pig wasn't real. The very idea of it was nuts. About as nutty as a witch-bone.

"You can come out now!" she announced to the others.

"Did you whack it? I didn't hear any *whackage*."

But there was nothing to whack. There was only—

"GRRRRrrrrrrr!"

As soon as Willa let her guard down, a furry beast screeched out of the darkness, lunging for her neck! It was too big to be Chubs. But maybe the witch-bone made things bigger after it brought them back. The reason didn't much matter. All that mattered were the vampire fangs about to tear a chunk out of Willa's throat!

She dropped to the ground and rolled, trying to shake loose the dead-alive thing. "Chubs, stop, it's me!" Up close, Willa clearly saw the green glow of its pointy teeth and the syrupy goop matted to its brown fur. *Grrrrrrr!* And the sales tag attached to its ear.

*WHAT?*

Willa stopped struggling and sat up straight. Why on earth would an undead guinea pig need a barcode? Unless...

In the same moment, she knew the thing in her hands wasn't Chubs or any other such creature. It was a stuffed animal, refitted with plastic vampire fangs and fake blood. It had performed its attack by 'flying' on a fishing line, an old special effects trick.

The culprit was laughing behind a tree. It was Billy, holding a fishing rod, his tiny sound effect gizmo attached to the rod. He was smiling from ear to ear. "Got ya!"

Willa vaulted to her feet. This time, he had gone too far.

# CHAPTER SIX

But not as far as Willa would go when she got hold of him. Billy would be dead. Deader than Chubs. "You little jerk! When I catch you…"

But Billy looked more confused than afraid. "What? You didn't think that was chill?"

By then, the girls had marched out of the tent, forming a united front behind Willa. "No, I didn't think it was *chill*. And I don't think Dad will think it's so chill when he finds out you were using his new fishing rod. And I don't think Mum will think it's so chill when she finds out who dug up her vegetables!"

"I didn't touch Mum's veggies!" shouted Billy.

But Willa was too upset to listen. "Let's go. We're waking them up right now!"

"But… but Dad likes to sleep in on weekends."

"That's right. So he'll be even madder!" She placed him in an armlock, a move she'd perfected on Tim.

Billy was starting to quiver. He looked so pathetic, in fact, that even Willa's friends took pity. "Hey, Will, lighten up. It was just a prank," Kayla said.

"Yeah. Like something you might have done," added Cassidy, "only better."

"You think so, huh? You think I'd do something as

disgusting, as *low*, as what he did the same day my pet died? Then you're more pathetic than he is. All of you! You're about as pathetic as that stupid witch-bone! If I had one more wish to make, I'd wish you'd leave. All of you. Go home!" Thunder struck, adding an exclamation point.

Cassidy, Tanisha and Kayla didn't respond. And really, what else was there to say? They marched back into the tent, grabbed their sleeping bags and left.

Willa watched them leave without a word. Yes, she'd lost her cool. But before you go critiquing our lead, remember: it had been an unusually lousy day.

Now there were only Willa and Billy, alone in the garden. He said nothing, either out of respect or intimidation. He picked up the skillet and handed it to his sister, not knowing whether or not she'd be whacking him with it but accepting the consequences all the same. "Sorry, Sis," he said with a whimper.

Wow! Can you believe it? Billy apologised. He actually said he was sorry. Also, can you believe somebody actually calls their sister 'Sis'?

Well, Willa didn't believe it. Not a word. It was just another one of Billy's ploys. He had to keep her from blowing the whistle to Mum and Dad. *Nice try, doofus.* But then she heard a different sound, this one not courtesy of his sound effects gizmo. Willa heard crying. Real crying, from her baby brother, something she hadn't had to deal with in a very long time. *Mustn't weaken now, Willa. Be strong. Don't back down. The weak get eaten.* So she simply enquired, "What's with you?"

"Nothing, jerkoid!" Oh, she had seen that coming. She could have seen it coming from a hundred miles away. But when Billy went sulking off with his head hanging, she chased after him. *Oh, no you don't. There's no way you're playing the victim card tonight.* This time, Billy slipped out of her hold. "Okay, tough guy, why the tears? What are *you* crying about?"

She didn't expect an answer, at least not a legit one. Something more along the lines of *I'm crying about your face, jerkoid!* But that's not what she got. You see, Billy had a solid reason for crying. His tears had been earned, the same as Willa's. He was crying for... "Chubs," Billy sniffled.

Willa crossed her arms and stared at her brother. "Chubs. Okay. So you're crying for Chubs." She thought about it. She couldn't let him get away with that one, either. "Crying for Chubs? You hardly looked at him when, well, when he was alive."

And that's when the real waterworks began. Billy started to weep. "Because you stole him from me!"

"What?" Willa was appalled. "Why would you say that? I never stole a thing from you… not ever!"

"Yes, you did. Chubs was my pet. *My* Christmas present. I loved him and you took him away. You took him from my room and you never even asked. Never even said you were sorry! Not ever! I hate you, Willa! Not ever!"

"Billy, I didn't know."

He stomped off once more, Willa's attempt at an apology coming too late. The damage was done – Billy was hurt; her friends were gone; Chubs was still deader than dead. Like her mum had said that morning, good times for all.

Now there was nothing left but to clean up. Willa might have waited until morning, but she couldn't sleep. She was a terrible sister, and just as bad a friend. The next day she would apologise. She would make it up to all of them. Starting with Billy.

She began dismantling the tent, yanking the first stake out of the ground.

*Rrrrreeeeech!*

It was that sound again. *Give it a rest, doofus!*

Willa removed the second stake.

*Quark! Quark!* That one sounded more like a bird. Courtesy of Billy's sound effects, no doubt.

She loosened the third stake. Suddenly, the noises converged, building to a crescendo of inhuman squeals, echoing from somewhere out there. Out where? **Come now, you know where.**

And so did Willa. She dropped the stake and picked up the lantern. She had to check it out. To give Billy the satisfaction of giving her one last scare, if that was what he needed. She probably deserved it, too.

She moved through the garden past the mangled veggies, the lantern illuminating her path. Willa arrived at the pet cemetery and tilted the light to get a better view. Chubs's grave was exactly how Billy had left it. She swung round, bringing light to the three remaining graves. *Uh-oh.* Those were not how she last saw them. They had been excavated. **That, in the cemetery trade, is the proper way of saying that they had been dug up and moved.** Pretty low, even for Billy.

Just then, a gentle breeze rattled Willa's charms. *Clink.* Goldie the goldfish. *Clink.* Rudy the rabbit. *Clink.* Polly the parrot. They had all been Willa's pets before Chubs arrived – on a Christmas morning as a gift for Billy.

*Wait a minute: Chubs was Billy's pet!*

And then Willa thought back to the witch-bone. To the exact wording she'd used: *I wish my pets could be alive again. My pets.*

And just as Willa completed her thought, she turned to see them advancing towards her: the zombified remains of a ravenous rabbit, a petrified parrot and a gruesome goldfish. Her undead pets swarmed her from head to half toe. Willa couldn't fight them off. They were pecking! Chewing! Slurping!

You see, Willa's pets hadn't eaten in years. Not since the last time she'd fed them, and they were very, *very* hungry…

# Chapter Seven

**W**illa was still staring at her bracelet when the old librarian looked up from the page. "Hmm. That one had *bite*. Critiques? Comments?"

This time there were none. At least, none that were vocalised. But Willa didn't like what she'd heard, not one bit. Or is it bitten?

"I'm done," she said. "I want to leave. Right now!" Usually, Tim would be the first to follow. But he'd been permanently... benched.

Willa took the initiative, snatching the candelabrum from the mantel. She searched high and low for a way out, finding nothing but bookshelves. She craned her neck, looking up at the ceiling. There was a skylight. She could hear rain pitter-pattering against the glass.

She slid the ladder underneath. "I'm a good climber. We can get out through there."

The librarian shook his head with mock despair. "Permanently sealed, I'm afraid, by Mistress Constance on her wedding night. The glass is reinforced. Unbreakable. Drafts, you know. They're magic carpets for bacteria."

But there had to be a way out, and Willa was determined to find it. She carried the candelabrum into the shadows where they'd first arrived. "We were here," she reasoned. Willa looked back at Noah and Steve for confirmation. As previously mentioned, Tim was still benched. But the other boys had nothing much to say, either. None of it made sense. Willa was pushing against a solid wall. "There's a passageway, I know it." She made a fist and gave the wall three good thumps.

She waited a second. And wouldn't you know it? Something *thump-thump-thump*ed back. "Who's there?"

"More like *what's* there?" questioned Noah.

The librarian expounded, "The foundation is constantly settling. Or is it *unsettling*? I never do get that right."

Willa was ready to explode! "That wasn't the foundation and you know it! Somebody knocked. I know a knock when

I hear one." And Willa thought, *Where there's knocking, there are people. And where there are people, there's...*

"Heeeelp!" She cried out to whoever might be listening. But Willa's voice didn't carry. It simply died right there in the room.

Willa would not accept defeat. She went back to Tim, her old standby, and knelt eye to eye with him. "I'm going to climb that shelf, Tim-bo." She pointed to the tallest bookcase. "I just need a boost." Willa reckoned she could make it all the way to the top and signal for help.

Unfortunately, Tim was in no condition to give a boost to anyone, not even his best pal. Before Willa could ask, Noah and Steve stepped over to volunteer. Joining her at the base of the bookcase, they interlaced their fingers and gave Willa a lift. The librarian watched, doing nothing to deter them.

Determined as ever, Willa made it to the very peak of the bookshelf, the skylight an arm's length away. It had some sort of antique crank on it. Willa stretched, clasping the lip of the bookcase with her left hand while managing to crank open the skylight with her right. The chill night air entered the library. *So the skylight can open,* she thought.

Some rain sprinkled Willa's face. She opened her mouth, startled. But the taste was amazing. It tasted like freedom.

She offered her friends a final thumbs up and climbed through the opening, Noah and Steve watching as Willa's legs vanished into the night.

In exactly two seconds, a figure appeared in the library, shuffling past Noah and Steve. It was Willa. "Will?" said Steve. She was somehow back where she had started, the skylight once again perfectly sealed. Willa paused, realising at once where she was but not questioning how she'd got there. It seemed all paths led back to the mansion. The librarian offered his most reassuring smile, which wasn't very reassuring at all.

"Your tale is finished, Mistress Willa," the librarian said.

She nodded, too numb to question his meaning.

"It's my turn, right?" Noah was doing the talking, often a brave soul when he had to be. And like Willa, he was starting to understand the rules. He pointed to Steve. "You said he goes last. That means I'm next."

"You're learning, Master Noah." The librarian flipped to the next story. And with Tim, Willa and Steve receding into the background, Noah became the star of his very own whopper of a fish story…

133

# Chapter Eight

## SEA CREATURES

# The swimming pool was unswimmable.

Noah guessed as much based on the gnarly thing draped over the above-ground structure. A tarp of metallic silver, like the stuff spacesuits were made from, littered with unidentifiable patches of greenish and purplish mildewy muck. What lay beneath was anyone's guess. Actually, Noah's guess was a mixture of fungi and weeds and water so rancid even his stepfather's dog wouldn't drink it. And let's face it: that damn dog drank anything. So, going back to where we started...

The swimming pool was unswimmable.

That made the task of cleaning it out all the more

terrifying. And not terrifying in a 'book featuring kids in a haunted mansion' sort of way. We're talking real-life terror.

This was exactly the kind of thing that always happened when Noah's mum went away on business. She was in some foreign country where they mostly spoke French. Very possibly France. He knew that because for the last two months, her *Learn French Fast* CD was the only thing coming out of the car speakers. *Parlez-vous français?*

*Le* nope.

That meant Noah would be stuck in the house with Philip and his ill-tempered poodle, Dots. Philip was Noah's stepfather, and before you go jumping ahead of yourself, yes, it's true: the uncaring step-parent is a common literary trope. A total cliché. Well, here's another total cliché for you: *Clichés are clichés for a reason.* And Philip fit the description of the uncaring stepfather to a tee.

Philip was a legend in his own mind, often rambling non-stop about his days in the service, the places he'd been, the things he'd seen, as if this automatically made him a hero. Perhaps he was a hero to his damn dog, but as Noah could tell you, Philip was anything but a hero to *him*. Certainly never hero enough to throw a ball around on a sad summer day. Or read a story before bedtime, like real fathers do.

Goodnight, moon. Goodnight, Dad.

**Break out the tissues, dear reader. For Master Noah's story starts as a sad one. But do not despair: those same tears will soon be running red...**

Noah's real dad had died when he was a lot younger. Like toddler young. But not young enough for Noah to forget him. Noah Gilman Sr was his dad's name, which is why Noah's mum sometimes referred to him as Junior. A decorated firefighter, Noah's dad had died helping others, something a real hero often does but seldom talks about. All that remained were the pictures and articles to prove it, and a gold plaque proudly displayed over Noah's bed.

Some of Noah's earliest memories were shrouded in fog, but he could still hear his dad's laugh and still picture him doing his long out-of-date dance moves in the den with Mum.

Philip never danced with Mum.

Mostly Noah remembered the day he received that plaque. It was the same day he was told his dad wouldn't be coming home again. Not ever.

**So now that we've cheered you up, let's get back to the saga of the unswimmable swimming pool.**

The pool had come with the house. And the house itself had come with Philip and his dog. It was all part of the deal, one predicated on Philip's marrying Mum. With the summer season just round the corner, Philip demanded Noah get the pool in shape under the false pretence that it provided a healthy alternative to sitting around reading horror stories. Noah had to admit his weight had become an issue. He had got good at ignoring the remarks made at school, but ignoring them doesn't mean you don't hear them. Besides, he had no choice. With Mum away, his stepfather was in charge.

"Laps," said Philip.

"Laps," repeated Noah, having no idea what that meant.

Philip explained that doing laps was the ultimate exercise. Better than going to a gym. "Once the pool's up and running, that flab will be a thing of the past." Philip patted Noah's belly. The remark might have hurt, had Noah really cared what his stepfather thought. And the funny part was Philip was sporting an above-average gut himself. The day Noah made the mistake of pointing it out, Philip impatiently explained that with middle age came girth.

So each day, starting at dawn, Noah headed to the garden armed with a mop, an old toothbrush and an assortment of cleaning products for the start of what would surely prove to be the worst summer ever.

Bedtime was the only time Noah looked forward to.

# CHAPTER EIGHT

Bedtime was *his* time. He had a treasure trove of fantasy and wonder stashed under his bed. There was a box containing his real father's collection of vintage horror comics, with titles like *They're Coming to Eat You* and *They Ate You Before They Left*.

Noah carefully removed each issue from its protective slip, reliving every garish tale, even the ones he knew by heart, as if it was the first time he'd ever laid eyes on it. If we're being honest, Noah even borrowed a few of the plot lines for the Fearsome Foursome. A personal favourite involved a miserable stepfather eaten by his stepchildren, who also happened to be werewolves. He must have read that one twenty times!

But that night, as he was leafing past the merchandise section, a particular advertisement caught Noah's eye. Now, if you've never seen one of these old horror comics, they're loaded with unusual things you can order by mail. Stuff like Venus flytraps – living plants that munch on insects. And X-ray glasses. And buzzers that stay hidden in your palm for a surprise handshake. But the one that had him salivating the most featured an illustration of an ancient sea creature, all tentacles and eyes. The ad claimed it belonged to a species that existed before the time of the dinosaurs. Noah didn't really believe all that. The ads always said those sorts of things to get you to buy stuff.

# THE FEARSOME FOURSOME

THEY'RE REAL! THEY'RE ALIVE! JUST ADD WATER AND WATCH THEM GROW! Pretty awesome. All you had to do was mail a cheque or money order for $2.95 to the Eldritch Company. Noah's heart started racing when he first saw the order form. It had already been filled out... in his name! But how could...

Noah soon realised it was *also* his father's name. *Uh-duh!* His dad must have planned on ordering sea creatures back when he was a kid. What had stopped him? Maybe he was short the $2.95. Or maybe he had no clue what a money order was, just like Noah. One thing was certain: the order form had never been mailed.

Noah got to thinking: wouldn't it be something if he could place the same order today? The Eldritch Company. Did it still exist? And would it continue to offer sea creatures in its back catalogue of dreadful delights? Noah pictured a giant warehouse filled with man-eating plants, fake vampire blood, monster masks and, yes, huge tanks overflowing with nearly extinct monstrosities.

Maybe it was the time of night. Or the fumes from the unswimmable swimming pool. But Noah decided it was worth a shot. Using his calculator, which Noah was amazed to find had an actual purpose outside of boring maths lessons, he adjusted the price for inflation, stuffed his dad's original order form into an envelope and sent it off to the Eldritch Company by snail mail, appropriately enough.

Later that night, Noah dreamt. He dreamt of his father. But when he woke up, there were no real details to cling to. Only a feeling. Like something bad was about to go down.

The next two weeks passed like treacle. Noah felt every second of every minute of every hour. By then, he was nearing the final stages. He had already gone to Pools 4 Fools and picked up the chemicals. Now for the fun part: filling the pool with water. Noah secured the garden hose and twisted the tap, the initial wave blasting across the lining like the birth of a new ocean. If all went according to plan, by the next day he'd be doing cannonballs... um, laps.

But the next day was a long way off.

The sliding door whipped open and out zipped Dots. The damn dog would have been bad enough, but Noah knew only too well, where there was Dots, there was Philip.

A second later, out pranced the general, waving a receipt like it was a losing lottery ticket. "What is this? What is this?" Noah instantly recognised it as the receipt from Pools 4 Fools. So he responded, "It's the receipt from Pools 4 Fools."

"Why?"

Noah wasn't sure he understood the question, but as

Philip demanded well-thought-out explanations, he gave one a shot. "Uhhh… because they give out receipts when you buy something?"

Philip's face turned beetroot red before graduating to aubergine purple. Even Dots stopped yapping, anticipating what the next vegetable might be. "Says here you bought chemicals. Pool supplies! Chlorine! Shock treatment! With my money!"

"I-I-I thought—"

Philip cut him off mid sentence. "You thought? You *thought*? Well, you thought wrong, cheesecake! Chlorine went out with the furry dinosaur! These days, healthy pools require salt water. Every idiot knows that!" He leant in, nose to nose with Noah. "Repeat after me: salt water, salt water, salt water!"

"Salt water," said Noah, adding the word *taffy* under his breath.

Apparently, salt was the new alternative for unswimmable swimming pools, something the part-time dude at Pools 4 Fools had neglected to mention.

"You do know what tomorrow is, don't you?"

"Yes, sir, the Fourth of July."

"And what's the Fourth of July, cheesecake?"

Noah wondered if that was a trick question. "I'm going with… Independence Day?" He saluted an imaginary flag.

Philip saluted, too, but that wasn't the response he was looking for. "It's also the unofficial official start of summer. I promised Dots we'd be the first to try out the pool." Noah's heart sank. The indignity. Philip never ceased to amaze him. But there was more. Philip always had more. "I picked up matching swimming trunks." He held up matching suits – one for him, one for Dots. "Adorable, no?"

Noah was about to vomit.

Philip trotted back to the house. "Make sure that salt gets in there, pronto. We're counting on you, cheesecake. Dots and me." Dots leapt dutifully into Philip's arms and they returned to the air-conditioned house, sealing the sliding glass door – heaven forbid some cool air sneak its way over to Noah.

Disheartened but not surprised, Noah wheelbarrowed the chemicals into a tool shed in the back. So Philip would be joining Dots for the official first swim of the season. In a pool *Noah* had suffered to make swimmable. Typical. But what were his options?

Noah returned to the pool shop to purchase everything required for a saltwater pool. And by late afternoon, the unswimmable swimming pool was up and running.

Noah was hot and exhausted. He had sunburn on his sunburn and more bug bites on his legs than his calculator could calculate. He moped to the front garden in a direct path to the sprinkler, where he planned to soak for about three days.

And that's when he spotted it.

An oversized manila envelope was leaning against the front door. He leapt from the sprinkler and snatched it up, then tore off to his room, dripping wet. It was addressed to Noah Gilman Sr and the return label said THE ELDRITCH COMPANY.

Noah locked his door. There could be no interruptions. This was big! He slit open the seal with his dad's penknife without noticing the antiquated postmark. It was dated twenty years earlier.

A small pouch marked ONE slid out onto the bed. It read LIVE EGGS. Whatever it was, it felt like granulated sugar. Noah shoved his hand inside the envelope, feeling around for pouch two – the one that supposedly contained the 'secret growthing serum', all of which sounded very mad scientist-like to Noah.

A folded slip of paper, yellowed with age, floated onto the bed. Noah hoped it would include some cool pictures instead of just words. All he got was the illustration from the ad. Underneath, it read *Welcome to the Ancient Past! To a Time Before Dinosaurs! To a World Dominated by Sea Creatures!*

Noah skimmed the directions.

*Pour contents of pouch one into clear water. Stir gently. Live sea creature will hatch. Add secret growthing serum. Watch hatchling grow!* At the very bottom of the page there was a warning, emboldened in what used to be red: *DO NOT USE SALT WATER!*

All Noah needed was a tank to grow it in. He remembered seeing an old fishbowl in the shed. He jumped up to go grab it, whipping open the door.

Philip was standing in the hall, hands on his hips, wearing look number one. By then, Noah had identified the three looks of Phil. One: angry. Two: gravely disappointed. Three: buffet-style hungry.

"Who traipsed water through my living room? I found footprints leading to your room. Explain!" This opening salvo indeed seemed to support look number one.

Noah thought about lying, but that was never his way. Instead, he answered with the truth. He'd forgotten to dry off after running through the sprinkler.

"Thanks for being honest." That went easy. But Philip

had more. He always had more. "By the way, your mother called."

Noah's face lit up. "Mom? When?"

"Hmm. I *honestly* forgot to tell you. Think about that. Think about it when you're mopping up that mess you made." Philip did an about-turn, and Noah could almost see the gaping grin through the back of his skull as he walked away. Dots lingered an extra moment, adding a snarky yap before scurrying after her master.

Noah stood there, steaming. A full-blown tantrum was in order, but he knew it would only worsen his situation. He opened his window for some air. And from there, he saw the glimmering, glassy reflection of the pool. Crystal clear, kudos to him… as if it actually mattered. All those days of hard work he'd never get back, and for what? There had to be something he could do. He wasn't a spiteful person, but hadn't Noah earned a little payback? He thought about the sea creatures. The warning about the salt water. And in that moment, Noah decided to do what you were already thinking he would.

You've got an evil little mind, don't you? My compliments.

He couldn't risk trying anything in the daytime. He would have to wait until after dark.

And that's precisely what he did.

Noah sneaked into the garden like he was on a stealth ninja mission, careful not to make a sound, lest Philip or his yapping sidekick wake up and foil his plans. He tiptoed to the side of the pool and was ready to begin the task when... a light flickered on!

Noah closed his eyes. Busted! Slowly, he pivoted to face...

... no one.

It was a mounted floodlight, tripped by a motion sensor. Noah continued the mission, now with the aid of some serendipitous mood lighting. He tore open pouch one, licking his lips as he imagined what it might do. Probably turn what was left of Philip's hair Willa blue. And he'd deserve it, too. He deserved whatever he got.

Noah sprinkled the contents into the water. Minute granules sparkled like pink diamonds in the moonlight. Cool to look at, but hardly the eggs of an ancient amphibious race as the ad had described. So much for truth in advertising.

Next he added the secret growthing serum, swirling it around with his finger, hoping the eggs would hatch. Probably not. Twenty years was a long time. But oh, if they did! Philip would be in for a July Fourth celebration right there in his matching swimming trunks. Boy, would he ever! Because as the ad also promised... *they bite.*

Noah didn't have to wait long for a monstrous reaction.

"Cheesecake, what's going on out there?" Philip's face was mushed up against his bedroom window. "It's almost midnight! Do you have any idea what time I wake up in the morning?"

Noah decided, on the heels of their last encounter, that honesty might not be the best policy. So he went with a little fib, telling Philip he was checking the pH balance to ensure the pool's safety for the next day. "Just looking out for you and Dots."

"All right, then. Get your big butt back to bed."

"Yes, sir!" said Noah.

Philip kept watch from his window as Noah marched back inside. As much as he wanted to, Noah couldn't look back at the pool. Not at the risk of spoiling the next day's surprise.

And what of the unswimmable pool? There was an eruption near the drain. Not an explosion of devastating proportions in and of itself, but the resultant manifestation would prove far more terrible. A singular white-hot tumour rose to the surface, followed by a second and a third, multiplying exponentially until the entire pool resembled a raging, primitive sea. It was volcanic upheaval, the granules splitting and re-forming, evolving and devolving into a shapeless mass. Something was about to be born. Something ancient. Something inhuman.

Something with an appetite.

# Chapter Nine

I t was just before two when the thing inside the pool took Dots. She had slipped outside as Noah was coming in, and spent the next hour and a half growling at the ancient whatever-it-was.

Noah was in bed. He had just managed to close his eyes when he heard the pathetic yelp. He got up and checked the window.

The pool was shrouded by fog. He could have sworn he saw something stirring just below the surface. A shadow flickered across his face, and he heard a firm *ker-plunk*. Noah wasn't imagining things. Something *was* in the water. And it had taken Dots for a moonlight swim.

Before he could consider what he was doing, Noah slipped on his flip-flops and flew out into the garden.

The floodlight popped on before he could make it to the pool. In the veiled light, Dots appeared to be hovering over the centre of the water, and the first thought that went through Noah's mind after his initial relief was, *How is she floating?* She wasn't, of course. Something was holding her up. Through the mist, he saw what appeared to be a translucent fire hose; it was wrapped round Dots's belly, lifting her an inch or so above the water. On closer inspection, Noah saw that the 'hose' was undulating with organic life. It was a squid-like tentacle, thick and bulging. What was worse: he could only imagine what the rest of it might look like.

Dots eyed Noah, and for the first time, she wasn't barking. She was too busy shivering. It was no secret that Noah didn't much care for Dots, but that was only because the damn dog didn't much care for him first. That's usually the only reason you dislike a dog: because it didn't like you first. Still, it was hard seeing her so helpless. So petrified. He even missed her cringe-inducing yelp, because Dots wasn't doing any yelping now. She knew enough not to upset that thing in the pool. For the moment, Noah was her only hope.

He looked around for potential distractions, anything to

save Dots from a fate too terrible even for her. The pool net was leaning against the shed, and it had an eight-foot ratchet pole. Noah snatched it and made his way back to the water. With a little coordination and a whole lot of luck, he might be able to lift Dots to safety before the creature even knew she was gone – no fuss, no muss.

Noah squatted down near the rim. Not too close, mind you. He still didn't know what he was dealing with. What special powers the creature might possess.

Dots saw him coming and wagged her tail in silent understanding. She agreed with the plan.

The net touched down, skimming the surface of the water until it found its way to her front paws. Perfect. All Dots had to do was hop on board and Noah could lift her out. She'd most likely take a nip at his ankles, but he'd worry about that later.

For the moment, he felt a strong connection to the dog – and she to him. If they got through this, if they somehow survived the night, maybe they could start afresh. Become pals. Go for walks. Play Frisbee. He might even clean up her poop. (All right, before we get carried away, he had to rescue her first.)

Her front paws stepped onto the net. *Keep going, girl,*

*you're halfway there.* Only the hind legs to go and Dots would be home free.

And she almost made it, too.

Until about five thousand gallons of salt water began shifting beneath her. The creature was aware of the rescue mission and was none too happy. A newly born tentacle sprouted from somewhere under the water, and from that, smaller ones squirted in all directions like tendrils of play string. One of the smaller appendages found the net and whisked it from Noah's hand. He could only watch, slack-jawed, as it twisted the pole into a metallic pretzel and whisked it over a fence, directly into the neighbour's garden.

Even more tentacles were starting to form. Thin ones, fat ones, some with hair. Others the length of beanstalks, all with undulating suckers – all searching for Noah!

He backed onto the patio, once again tripping the floodlight. The concealing fog had begun to dissipate, affording Noah his first real look at the hideous newborn in the unswimmable pool. It was enormous, taking up every square inch of the twenty-four-foot round container. Like a terrifying experiment in nature gone wrong, it had no defining shape, for it was ever evolving. Its colour, too, was ever changing, blending in with its environment, so you'd never see it coming… until it was too late. It really was the perfect monster. It could form arms when it wanted to grab you, acquire eyes when it saw fit to see you, grow sharp teeth when it needed to eat you. It was unlike anything any human being had ever seen before… and lived to talk about.

Noah had to come up with an alternate plan and come up with it fast. He remembered seeing a pitchfork in the garage, but that idea seemed prone to extreme messiness, and it didn't take a genius to know who'd be assigned the clean-up. The pool ladder, however, was available; nice and light, easy to manage. And long enough to keep some distance between him and the creature.

Noah lifted the ladder as Dots awaited his arrival. Unfortunately, the creature was also waiting. Noah poked at some blubbery limb posturing just below the surface, hoping to divert its attention away from its canine hors d'oeuvre. This only made the creature irritable. (So we have *that* in common. Sea creatures, like people, get completely annoyed when you poke 'em with ladders!)

And when sea creatures get annoyed, they emit a supersonic sound that can shatter glass, which is exactly what occurred.

*EEEEEEEEEEEEEEEK!*

Noah covered his ears, and right behind him, the sliding glass door exploded into a billion shards. Of course, he instantly knew who'd be cleaning *that* up.

Obviously, there would be no reasoning with this creature. Its rage knew no bounds; its slithery feelers whipped haphazardly in all directions, looking for something to grab. The ad claimed it hailed from a time before the dinosaurs. As he stared into the pool, Noah couldn't help wondering if this wasn't the thing that had *ended* the dinosaurs. If it ever got out, if it somehow left the garden, it would overtake the neighbourhood. If it kept on growing... it could very likely take over the world.

Speaking of blobs of thoughtless hostility... Philip emerged from the empty rectangular space that used to be the sliding door, firing off a litany of words not suitable for printing. "What's going on out here? Where's my door? Do you know what time it is? Where's Dots?" That is the abridged version, by the way (with apologies to Willa).

Noah stood there, speechless. He had both nothing and everything to say. In this case, a visual seemed more effective. So he pointed. "Over there," he managed to say.

Philip whistled for his sidekick. "Dots! Come here,

girlie... girl... girl! Come to Daddy!" He looked to Noah for an explanation. "Well, where is she?"

"Inside the pool, sir." Noah had to tell him. "With... that."

As Philip moseyed over, the creature swiftly retreated below the surface – totally gone from sight. Philip glanced into the water, noticing only a few innocuous ripples. "With what, cheesecake? Learn to articulate!"

"Don't get too close!"

Ignoring Noah's warning, Philip leant over the rim. "Dots!" He spotted her right away, and he must have seen the other thing, too, because Philip switched over to mute. No yelling, no cursing. And then something happened that Noah hadn't expected. A new voice emerged, one filled with emotion. Philip was calling to Dots the way Noah imagined a real father might call to his kid. And in that moment, he no longer hated his stepdad. True, true, he wasn't about to run out and buy him a card, but it was sort of a relief to know that the creep who had married his mum had a heart after all... even if it was about to get eaten.

A beefy tentacle slunk out of the pool, and before Philip knew what was happening, it lassoed round his waist, lifting him straight up into the air for a free ride over the garden. He must have been thirty feet high.

Dots craned her head and watched like it was the fireworks pre-show. For the grand finale, Philip came plummeting down into the centre of the pool. *KER-PLUNK!* The world's biggest belly flop.

How delightfully it all worked out. Philip and Dots really did manage that first swim after all. Pity it might be their last.

Philip found himself entangled in a virtual garden of living appendages, although he did receive a small measure of comfort when Dots made it back into his arms. Reunited and it felt so good… if you considered being in the clutches of a giant prehistoric tentacle a good thing.

The creature took them for yet another spin, Philip and Dots whipping around the pool like toys in a bathtub. As they whizzed past Noah, he could hear Philip's voice pleading: "Help us, Son! You have to help us!"

*What? No 'cheesecake'?*

Of course, technically, Noah didn't have to do a thing. He could pull up a chair, sit back and enjoy the show. And for like a millionth of a second, that's pretty much what he considered doing. If it got Philip and Dots out of the way, that nameless monstrosity might be the answer to his prayers. As they say on those *Learn French Fast* CDs, bon appétit!

But when that millionth of a second had passed, Noah knew in his heart that leaving them to perish was never an option. For the first time in his life, he understood who he was. Noah was his father's son. For the sake of the name he carried so proudly, there was no way he could take the coward's way out now.

Almost immediately, his fear was replaced with a sense of purpose. Sure, about a second and a half later, the fear came back, but still, what a grand second and a half it was! He was going to save them – somehow. And Noah told them so. "Hold on! I'll think of something!"

"We'll wait," replied Philip, unaware of how ridiculous that sounded.

Noah ran through a shopping list of anti-monster options. He could call the Eldritch Company, talk to their complaint department. All right, that was plain silly. By the time he got through, the creature would be on dessert, and besides, there really wasn't anything to complain about. On the contrary: that thing in the pool certainly lived up to the advertisement. Talk about getting your money's worth!

What about the police? Maybe get the military

involved? The Japanese army? They could deal with it. They'd dealt with prehistoric monsters before. But time was of the essence. Noah heard a gurgle from the pool, a sound he recognised. It was the same one his stomach made right before breakfast.

He got up on his toes, just in time to witness—

**With my most humble apologies, decorum prevents me from describing what he saw. It might cause nightmares for our more impressionable readers. On second thought, why not? We only die once. Here it goes:**

A wall of blubbery flesh split down the middle, revealing a gigantic maw just below Philip and his dog. It was a gargantuan mouth attached to a throat leading to the creature's pulsating empty stomach. The stench was that of an ancient world, where creatures such as those ruled the sea. There were plumes of steam rising from the newly formed orifice; its digestive acids were already beginning to brew, its fluids powerful enough to dissolve a car in minutes. For Philip and Dots, the suffering wouldn't last long. The stinging vapours would instantaneously dissolve them into pools of unidentifiable goo. And for the parts that didn't melt, the mouth had already begun to sprout teeth: layers upon layers of jagged fangs of varying lengths, some up to ten inches long!

**Well, you know what they say: Where there're teeth, there're tentacles. Okay, nobody says that. But as the segue to our next passage, it's dead on!**

A multitude of tentacles burst through the pool's lining, snaking their way under the grass like living roots. Noah would be dead meat if they caught him. He tried making a move for the house, but a wiggly wall of feelers was already there, anticipating his route.

He returned to the lawn, hopping over tentacles at every turn. The neighbour's fence was in range. He thought about giving it a shot, but at times like those, you had to recognise your own limitations, and Noah wasn't what you'd consider a gifted climber.

A whip-like tendril snapped near his ankles. Noah ran across the garden in a serpentine pattern, just barely avoiding capture. There was one other option – the metal tool shed. If he could make it inside, perhaps he could come up with a plan, because when you're running for your life, it isn't the best time for planning. When you're running for your life, you're mostly thinking: *Oh god, I'm running for my life!*

He took a breath and bolted for the shed. It wasn't very far, about twenty feet, but given the circumstances, it felt like twenty miles. Noah's flip-flops flew from his feet but he kept on going. No tears – they were from Dollar Duds. And in fact, they represented the best buck Noah had ever spent, because the tentacles, not being the sharpest extremities in the pond, busied themselves with his footwear, buying Noah just enough time to make it into the shed.

He closed the door and spun round, looking for something he could use as a barricade. There wasn't much to work with. An old lawnmower, entangled with webs. The pool supply bin. A ball of twine, which he used to tie the door handles together.

Then all he could do was listen. But what was there to hear? Things had turned awfully quiet in the garden. No more cries for help. No incessant yapping. Had the inevitable happened? Was the creature busy with breakfast? And how long before it started thinking about lunch?

Sometimes it isn't your fault. Sometimes you do everything right and, still, the cards are stacked against you. That's pretty much what happened to Noah. Because as quiet as he'd been, he hadn't anticipated the musical interlude that ultimately gave him away. It was a text alert. And if it wasn't the loudest rendition of 'Night on Bald Mountain' ever heard, it was enough of a vibration for an inquisitive sea creature to respond to.

Noah clicked the phone to silent but the damage had already been done. The text, by the way, was from Steve: NEED HELP ASAP. What help could he possibly need at that hour? Advice on which chick to take to the movies? While Noah was trapped inside a shed, fighting for his life? Bad timing, Steve-o. Still, Noah knew enough texting etiquette to punch in a quick response: CAN'T – BIGGER FISH TO FRY.

In the time it took to hit send, the steel roof had crumpled into a ball of tinfoil. Then came the gnashing as the walls folded in on themselves.

A thick grey tentacle slid in through the damaged roof, forcing Noah into the opposite corner, where he wedged himself between the lawnmower and the supply bin. As it oozed down the wall, the tentacle lifted the lawnmower like it was a feather, and crushed it with similar ease. But the most nauseating part had to be the suckers, those puckery thingamajigs you see on squids and octopuses. Except, unlike those of the creature's cephalopod cousins, these suckers had eyes. A bulbous black one erupted from the tip and was now searching for Noah. At first it couldn't find him, and Noah thought about giving it a good poke. But there was all that eye gunk to consider.

Instinctively, he reached into the supply bin, feeling around for something, anything, to defend himself with. What he needed was a military-grade bazooka. What he got was an inflatable frog float. *Ribbit ribbit.*

The eyeball saw the float and paid it no mind. The frightened lad who was holding it – now, that was its prize. The tentacle forged a deliberate path to Noah's bare feet, inching forwards in a worm-like rhythm. It was biding its time. The hunt was over, its prey was trapped and the sea creature wanted the human boy to embrace the terror of his own demise.

By now, you know the rules of being scared witless. Let's review. One: Noah froze in place. Two: Noah dropped the float. *Ribbit–plop.*

The tentacle slid under his foot and curled round his ankle. It was as cold and unforgiving as the sea. In an instant, it lifted Noah from the ground. It could just as easily have crushed him, but the sea creature preferred its sustenance alive and kicking and afraid. As it hoisted him towards the roof, Noah realised he had no one to blame but himself.

Spitefulness had led him there. Still, that wasn't the way he planned on going out.

With one last-ditch effort, Noah shoved his hand into the supply bin and came out with a fistful of white powder. Without thinking, he flung it into the monster's eye. *Grrrrrrrrrr!* It burned; it stung! The tentacle released Noah and started flopping about like it was on fire. *Clang! Clung! Cling!* It slammed into all four walls of its metal enclosure. Noah scurried back into the corner, watching in terror as the thick tentacle retreated through the broken roof.

He was thankful to be alive. Right away, he understood what had saved him. It was that powder! Noah checked the supply bin and saw the sack of shock treatment. As it turned out, the best weapon against ancient sea creatures was good old-fashioned chlorine! Not such a waste of Philip's money after all.

Noah sprung to his feet – *sprung* being a relative term. He now had a weapon, and it was time to wage war, Gilman-style.

Noah loaded the sack into the wheelbarrow. The creature's limbs had retreated back into the pool, where the nameless monstrosity felt safe. Noah wheeled the shock treatment across the garden, manoeuvring over and around the countless tentacle tracks engraved throughout the lawn.

Arriving poolside, he spotted Philip and Dots, their heads barely above water. Using a plastic shovel the part-time dude from Pools 4 Fools had thrown in for free, Noah began heaving the powder into the unswimmable swimming pool.

The reaction was swift and powerful. The sea creature wailed another supersonic boom – *EEEEEEEEEEEEEEEK!* – blowing out the remaining windows. Its tentacles thrashed aimlessly about, pounding the walls of the pool. Noah backed away, fearing it might burst.

It didn't.

The once mighty sea creature was now spinning out of control in an unrelenting whirlpool of its own creation. Noah watched with awe and perhaps a touch of pity. A change was taking place. The creature was shrinking right before his startled eyes, getting smaller, smaller, smaller... until it matched the illustration in the ad, in both size and appearance. With a final sucking sound, the ancient thing spiralled down into the pool drain, along with every last molecule of salt water.

And then there was silence as the first rays of sunlight entered the garden.

# CHAPTER NINE

Noah stood up as he listened to the first sounds of the day. The song of the morning bird. A lawnmower revving up next door. And children laughing. Those were the best sounds he knew. They were the sounds of summer.

Noah closed his eyes, soaking it all in... until he remembered. "Philip and Dots!" He retrieved the ladder and climbed to the top rung, peering down into the pool. The water was all gone. It was empty except for Philip, sitting by the drain, with Dots nestled in his arms. "You saved us. You're a hero." Philip got to his feet, extending his hand. "My hero."

Noah hesitated. Was this for real? Well, considering what he'd just been through, it was no less real than an ancient sea creature. Noah decided to go for it. He shook Philip's hand for the first time in about a year, and he had to admit it felt pretty good. But Philip wasn't done. He pulled Noah in for a hug, whispering, "I'm proud of you, Son," into his ear.

Now, in the interest of full disclosure, this wasn't the longest hug. And it wasn't even the warmest. But for Noah, it was a pretty great start.

And can you believe it? Dots – even Dots! – jumped up to give Noah a thank-you lick! Well, don't believe it. The damn dog still didn't like him. But from that moment on, things were going to change for the better around there. Philip even said the words: "From this moment on, things are going to change for the better around here."

Noah thought about his dad, and he smiled. He smiled about the past. And for once, he could smile about the future.

Noah smiled right up to the moment when a regenerated tentacle burst up from the drain and dragged him, kicking and screaming, into the deepest primordial recesses of the earth.

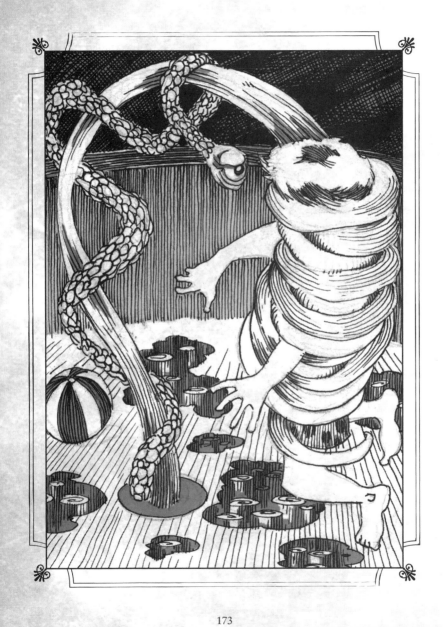

# Chapter Ten

**T**he librarian finished reading. "Shock treatment, indeed." He looked up from the page, eyeing the individual faces of the Fearsome Foursome. "Critiques? Comments?"

"Dumb," blurted Steve. He looked at Noah to see if he agreed.

"Dumb," repeated Noah before adding, "but… it's true about the pool. We're opening it next weekend." He winced as he touched a nasty patch of sunburn on his shoulder.

The librarian acquiesced. "A strange coincidence. Death imitating art. Or is it art imitating death? I never can get that right."

Like the others, Noah was demanding answers. "What do you want from us?" he shouted in a voice that would do Philip proud.

"What do I want? I thought I made that perfectly clear." The librarian made a sweeping gesture with his hand, alluding to his books. "Tales such as your own were meant to be heard."

At that point, the others were no longer looking for a way out. Not even Willa, a revelation which pleased the librarian no end. "You've decided to stay?"

"Do we have a choice?" Willa asked, already knowing the answer. She was nobody's fool. "None of us can leave until we hear the last story. That's how it works, isn't it?"

The librarian lit a candle and looked at them with a calm expression. "I suppose, I suppose."

Steve got up in his face. He was red with anger. Or maybe terror. "All right, old man, get it over with! Read mine!"

"Do I *dare*?" questioned the librarian, wearing a considerably sinister grimace, for the librarian was harbouring a grave secret all his own. Yes, they were nearing that part of the evening he enjoyed the most.

He opened to the final tale and began to read...

# Chapter Eleven

## THE DARE

**Y**ou've heard
the expression
'a fate worse than death'?

A fate worse than death. Think about that. It has to be pretty bad to beat dying. The eternal sleep. Kicking the bucket. Whatever they call it around your house. Let's indulge in a little list of what some of these fiendish delights might be.

Let's see... getting eaten alive. That should qualify. Whittled down to the bone by a shark, or a bear. Or worse, a school of hungry piranha. "Yum-yum."

How about a dip in boiling acid? Feeling the flesh melt from your bones. "Mind if I skip my bath tonight, Mother?"

Or paper cut torture. Hours upon hours of... well, I suppose that one's self-explanatory, right? There are countless fates worse than plain old death. Why not make a list of your own? Go on. We'll wait.

But near the top of everyone's list – at least for those of us who think about such things – is the terror of being buried alive. It has been since the beginning of human existence. Think about it for a moment. You wake up in a coffin. Can't see a thing. There is no light. You can barely move. It's a very tight fit. All there is to do, once you realise what's happening, is scream. And nobody can hear you – that is, except for the worms. And all you've done is save them the job of finding you. That would unequivocally be a fate worse than death.

# CHAPTER ELEVEN

It is also the subject of our final tale. Therefore, if you find the thought of being buried alive objectionable or the subject matter distasteful, by all means, go read Sallie's Silly Sewing Circle.

Still here, foolish reader? Very well, I warned you.

# THE FEARSOME FOURSOME

**S**teve, Steve, Steve. He had that reputation to protect. It might have been the wavy black hair. Or the roguish smile. Yet in reality, Steve never got into fights or did any of those things bad boys were generally known for. He didn't deny that he did them, either, which was how he kept his rep intact. The same way he didn't announce his loyalty to the Fearsome Foursome. The fact that Steve was a reader, and that he liked to invent stories, did not go hand in hand with being one of the cool kids. Or the king of dares, as he was known throughout the school.

What exactly is a king of dares? Well, it's not a position you're born into. Or elected to. It's a title you have to earn.

It started innocently enough, as a game to pass the time during break. Each day, students gathered for a round of 'I Dare You to...'. It's sort of like Truth or Dare, if you're familiar with that. The first player poses a challenge, which the other player has to decide whether or not to accept. The dares were usually pretty harmless (or dumb, take your pick). They ranged from hopping on one foot around the canteen to saying something borderline inappropriate to Ms Greene, the uptight health teacher. So far, no one had got into any real trouble. Although Andy Kenderson did receive an in-school suspension for picking his nose while placing his lunch order. Yet, it's important to note, Andy won the dare.

But this is Steve's story. Steve-o to his pals. The once and future king of dares. You see, Steve never backed away from a challenge. Not once. Not ever.

That is, until Roland Price moved to town. Now, we always hear how hard it is for a new kid entering a new school, but that wasn't the case for Roland, or Rolly, as he was known. It wasn't that he was particularly good at sports. Or that he was fast with a joke, or that he had the hottest looks. In any of those departments, Rolly Price could be generously described as average. But it was during break time that his true gifts came to the forefront. You see, Rolly Price had no fear – not of anything. It might have had something to do with moving around so much – eleven schools in eight years – but nothing scared him. Well, almost nothing. We'll get to that.

If you dared Rolly to swallow a worm, he'd do it and then make a yummy face, suggesting he liked it. Hopping around the canteen? Kids' stuff. Rolly once crab-walked into the headmaster's office to ask the time.

The kids at break hooted and cheered. Even Ellie, the petite cheerleader Steve had spent an entire term trying to woo, had officially declared Rolly the new king of dares.

Yes, Steve had been dethroned. Every challenge he threw Rolly's way was taken on and mastered. Staring contests, silent treatments, breath holding, musical note holding, eating, drinking, wedgies, nose picking – you name it. Rolly Price out-dared him at every turn. And that's what pushed Steve to a place he never should have gone. To the ultimate dare – a dare that would cost him more than his silly little title.

But first Steve needed to discover Rolly's weakness, if a weakness actually existed. He spent several days and nights racking his brains. What could it be? He tried everything there was to try and was at his wit's end when the fearful finger of fate intervened. Steve was by his locker just before the end of the school day when Tim ran over with the news. "You hear what happened to Rolly today? He got stuck in the caretaker's cupboard and totally freaked out."

At first Steve was concerned. "Is he okay?"

"Oh, yeah, he's fine. It was only for, like, a minute or two. But when the caretaker unlocked the door, Rolly flew out screaming. He could hardly walk – he didn't even know where he was."

"For real?"

"For real." And that was when Tim provided Steve with the gift he'd been looking for. "Rolly told the caretaker, get this, that he suffers from extreme claustrophobia!"

*Extreme claustrophobia. Yesssss!* Steve was giddy beyond words. Rolly Price had a weakness after all: a fear of tight spaces. Immediately, the wheels started turning. All he needed was the perfect dare, one Rolly couldn't complete even if he wanted to. A ghoulish idea entered Steve's mind. He had just the challenge. The perfect dare.

The next day during break time, the current king of dares was holding court by the swings. Steve had been spying from behind the bike sheds, and he saw Ellie laughing at one of

Rolly's recycled jokes and another dude nodding, as if Rolly really was the most popular kid in school. It was time to take him down. Like in the good old days, a king was about to be beheaded.

Steve approached the swings with a bit of the old swagger that usually got him noticed. Except that day, the only one who saw him coming was Rolly. "Yo, Steve-o. S'up?"

"Nothing but the sky, Rolly." Crickets. Not even a sympathy chuckle. Steve quickly dispensed with the pleasantries. "You up for a final round?"

The other kids scattered like it was the Old West and a shoot-out was imminent.

Rolly remained where he was, a king on his swinging throne. As cool as a corpse. "How many times, Steve-o? How many times you need to be defeated in public?"

"That mean you're scared?"

You could literally have heard a pin drop, but seriously, who brings a pin to break time? Rolly hopped down from the swing. He was smaller than Steve, but you wouldn't know it. Confidence made him a giant. "I suggest taking off before you lose what little rep you got left."

Steve shook his head. "Guess that means you really *are* scared."

If he was, Rolly didn't show it. "Name it. Right now. Throw down your best dare."

"I really don't think you could handle it, Roll. We all heard about the cupboard."

The others looked at Steve, and somebody yelled out, "Shots fired!" Steve gave Rolly a condescending pat on the head. From the corner of his eye, he saw Ellie climb down from the monkey bars. Steve must have had something 'real' in mind, or he wouldn't have posed the challenge in front of everyone. And Rolly wasn't stupid. He knew it would be based on his fear of tight spaces. But he also knew that if he chickened out, he'd lose everything he'd gained; he'd be nothing more than the new kid again.

Steve headed for the playground and Rolly followed, an entourage of students in tow. "On one condition!" Rolly declared.

Steve didn't slow up. "Oh, yeah? What's that?"

"Winner takes all. The loser has to admit defeat in front of the entire school."

"Naturally."

"And one more thing…"

Steve glanced over his shoulder. He could tell from the

smirk on Rolly's pudgy little face that he thought he had the deal breaker. "Name it."

"The loser has to publicly address the winner as His Royal Highness. Forever."

That made Steve laugh. "Fine by me. So? We ready to do this?"

By that point, the crowd had increased by exponential proportions. Kids seemed to be everywhere: standing on fences, piled on shoulders. How had that happened? Did they bus them in from other schools? Still, it was no skin off Steve's back. He welcomed an audience and proceeded with the formal introduction: "I dare you to…" He paused and the crowd leant in – those same kids who'd once thought him the coolest. And soon would again.

Rolly was all out of patience. "Well?"

Steve suppressed his smile. "I dare you to… spend one full hour locked in a coffin." Then came the smile. He knew he had the ultimate dare, and an audible gasp told him the crowd agreed. But Rolly's reaction – *that* was the kicker. His knees buckled. Just for a second, but long enough for Steve to notice.

Yes, he was afraid. Rolly Price was human, after all. "Yes or no? Do you accept the dare?" Steve demanded. Beads of sweat trickled from Rolly's forehead. Now the crowd was chanting: "Accept! Accept! Accept!"

Rolly thought about it. He thought, *Easy for them. They don't have to spend two seconds locked in a coffin, let alone one hour!* He knew he couldn't accept Steve's dare. Things had gone far enough already. But there's something about peer pressure that makes smart people do incredibly stupid things. And before Rolly knew what he was saying, the words, "I accept your dare," slipped off his tongue.

The crowd stopped chanting and Steve stopped smiling. That was unexpected. Upon hearing the dare, Rolly was supposed to melt into a glob of jelly. Mop him up, stick him in a jar and send him back to wherever he came from! But no. The new kid didn't back down. Not really.

"I accept. With one more condition."

"I thought there might be. Name it, buddy boy."

Rolly pulled out his trump card. "The coffin – it has to be real. Not that fake cardboard junk they sell at Parties 4 Smarties. If you can't provide a real, honest-to-goodness coffin, then your dare is a dud – a forfeit – declaring me the winner." Rolly had thrown the challenge back into Steve's lap. Real coffins were expensive, not to mention difficult to come by. There was no conceivable way a middle school kid could come up with a real one. But Steve was holding a wild card of his own. An ace in the hole. Like a skeleton in the grave.

"I got a real coffin."

Rolly saw at once that Steve wasn't bluffing. "H-how? W-what? W-where?" he stammered.

"My cousin Drew. He drives a hearse for the Davis Family Funeral Home." Rolly literally gulped. The 'literally' comes in because you rarely hear anyone gulp in real life. It's about as rare as a double take.

"I wouldn't want to get your cousin in any trouble," said Rolly. Kind of a weak retort.

"Let me worry about the Drew-meister. You just worry about showing up on time. This Saturday. After hours. Drew has total access. Including a coffin with your name on it."

Ellie snuggled up next to Steve, as if she'd always been there. The rest of the crowd shifted to his side of the playground. Once again, it was Rolly against the world. Steve extended his hand. "Saturday night we end this." They shook on it, sealing the dare.

For Steve, Saturday night couldn't get there fast enough, because all the preparations had been made. **What preparations? Oh, you'll find out. And you'll be sorry when you do.**

Well, Saturday night arrived – as it always does – and Steve found himself waiting outside the Davis Family Funeral Home, as arranged. The sign had just flickered off; they were closed for the evening. The funny thing about funeral homes is that most of them look like regular houses, where regular families might live. Except they aren't. This one was painted all white, with black shutters and matching trim. Not very menacing in the daytime. But daylight wouldn't be returning for another eight hours.

For now, there was only night.

Steve checked the time. Rolly was late, three whole minutes. Maybe he wouldn't show and the dare would be declared a forfeit. But Steve was hoping it wouldn't come to that. He needed Rolly to show. Oh, yes, foolish reader, this was going to be the dare – make that the scare – of the century.

Another minute passed and Steve grew anxious. It didn't help that those black shutters were now flapping, and what was that other sound? *Clump-clump-clump.* That one he couldn't explain. It must be nerves, and anyway, *where was Rolly Price?*

A hand crawled up Steve's back, then slithered insect-like along his shoulder blades. Steve didn't really want to turn, but he had to look. He slowly twisted his head to find… Rolly Price, all smiles, standing behind him. "Little jumpy there, Steve-o. What's the matter? Didn't think I'd show?"

Steve located his cool voice. "You're late." He pointed to the car park behind the funeral home. "Thataway. Back entrance." **Where the clients come to stay, though there's always room for one more…**

"Lead the way, Steve-o," said Rolly. And that's just what Steve did.

A company hearse was parked at the far end of the car park, next to a roped-off section where some construction had been going on. A rail-thin man in a chauffeur's uniform was leaning against the driver's door reading a newspaper. He glanced up as they rounded the corner, and acknowledged Rolly with a tip of his cap.

Rolly realised something: "That must be…"

"Cousin Drew," confirmed Steve. He pointed to the back entrance, shrouded by a black-and-white awning. Rolly hesitated. He had never been inside a funeral home before. He'd been lucky that way. On that night, his luck ran out.

They entered through a narrow corridor, which expanded into a waiting area. There were some cushiony chairs and a fancy red carpet. Oh, and the lights were kept low. No need for a hefty electric bill. The dead didn't require much light.

Steve pointed out the three doors leading to the separate viewing rooms. Rolly could guess what was behind them. Coffins, stuffed with dead folks! Steve tapped the sign in front of viewing room three. It read THE PRICE FUNERAL.

Rolly acted brave, with an emphasis on *acted*. "Oh, boy, that was unexpected." And actually, it was.

Steve unlocked the door and escorted Rolly inside. There were three rows of folding chairs facing a stage, and for a second, Rolly closed his eyes and made a silent wish: *Please, let it be a Taylor Swift concert*. But a concert wasn't on the agenda. At least, not one for the living. As they made their way down the centre aisle, Rolly's chest grew tight. The star of the show had revealed itself: an oblong box, made of polished steel, with a faux wood exterior. It was a real coffin, just like Steve had promised, lying horizontally on a wooden platform. The lid was open, inviting Rolly in.

Steve stepped onto a kneeling bench and looked inside. "Check it out, Roll. Your new home." In the same moment, the lights flickered: a power surge. "That wind's really acting up tonight," said Steve. Rolly wondered if that wasn't all a part of his grand scheme.

"Step right up, Mr Price," Steve said like a carnival

ringmaster. Rolly joined him on the bench. "What we have here is the Eternal Rest Deluxe Recliner."

"What do you mean? They name these things?"

"Of course they name them. They name everything. Cars, mattresses, hot wings. What we have here is the Rolls-Royce of coffins." He patted the inside. "Blue velvet interior. Matching throw and pillows. Fully adjustable bedding."

"Why?"

Steve didn't understand the question. "Why what?"

"Why's a dead guy need adjustable bedding?"

"They're in there forever." Steve displayed his best Fearsome Foursome smile. "You never know."

"Never know *what*?"

"When you need to adjust," Steve continued. "It's guaranteed not to rot for ten years."

Rolly raised his hand like he was in class. "Question: how would anybody know? I mean, does somebody inspect these things after they're buried?"

Steve shrugged; he hadn't thought about that. He slid his fingers under the lid, manoeuvring a stainless steel catch. "Reinforced lock." He clicked it into position with a reverberating *snap*. To Rolly, this seemed the strangest option of all. Again, he raised his hand.

"Question: why put locks on the outside? Are they worried a customer might crawl out and complain?"

Again, Steve flashed that ghoulish grin. This time with elaboration. "Don't think so. You see, regulation depth is six feet under the ground. Even if you could open the lock, you'd still have all that dirt to deal with. All that dark, wet, worm-infested earth weighing you down. Two tons of it between you and the surface. You'd be going nowhere fast, Roll. Unless you had super-strength. You don't have super-strength, do you?"

"The last time I checked, no."

"Didn't think so." Steve held up his mobile phone, setting a timer for exactly one hour. The moment of truth had arrived. He stepped down from the kneeling bench, inviting Rolly to take his place inside. "Ready to do this?"

Rolly lifted his leg to climb in. There was a natural hesitation. It wasn't the sort of thing one usually did voluntarily.

"Wanna quit?" Steve goaded him. "Last chance, buddy boy."

If Rolly had any doubts, Steve had just erased them. He lay flat inside the Eternal Rest Deluxe Recliner. Rolly had to admit it was pretty darn comfy.

Getting into the spirit of things, Rolly crossed his arms over his chest. Steve just shook his head. "I wouldn't do that. Once the lid goes down, it's a pretty tight squeeze. Folding your arms might constrict your breathing."

Rolly sat straight up. "Really? Did you have to say that?" He was sweating big time. All over the blue velvet interior.

Steve had him right where he wanted. "Ready to quit? I dare you to say the words… 'I quit'."

That seemed to do it. "I got some words for you, Steve-o." Rolly wiped off the sweat with his sleeve.

"Oh, yeah? What's that?"

"See you in an hour." He reached up to detach the safety bar that propped open the lid. Steve got to it first, the genial host. "Don't pull down on the safety bar. I will lower it for you." And that's what he did.

From inside the coffin, Rolly watched as the lid *slooooowly* came down, eclipsing the light. Now there was only darkness, Rolly's sole comfort being his own laboured breathing, amplified by the natural acoustics of the casket. That sound alone could drive one to madness. The intermittent puffs, growing smaller with each exhale. But being interred under the ground, that would be worse. Knowing that your loved ones were standing in their best shoes a mere six feet above you, unaware that you were still alive, and doing nothing to help out. As you lay there, boxed in like a sardine, with the knowledge that those cries you wasted used up what precious little air you had left. Oh, yes, that would clinch it. Being buried alive would be a fast pass to insanity.

"How we doing in there?" came a voice from the viewing room, interrupting Rolly's morbid musings. It was Steve-o, of course. "Comfy cosy?"

"You want to keep it down? I'm trying to catch a little shut-eye in here." Rolly sounded calm, and in fact, for a kid who had suffered an extreme panic attack in a caretaker's cupboard, he seemed uncommonly relaxed.

Steve snapped the lock in place, and in case Rolly had forgotten the sound, Steve cheerfully reminded him: "You're locked in. There's no escape. But the good news is a whole minute just went by. That means you only have fifty-nine more to go, buddy boy. I'm going to grab a smoothie. Want anything?"

"Strawberry-banana," replied the voice from inside the Eternal Rest Deluxe Recliner, and a thought flashed through Steve's mind: in the vast history of human existence, that might have been the only time the words *strawberry* and *banana* were said from inside a locked coffin.

Steve played a little drum solo on the lid. "You got it." He heard Rolly shifting inside, providing him with immeasurable delight. Drew had entered and was silently observing from the top of the aisle. He exchanged knowing looks with his cousin, and Steve's grin graduated from ghoulish to devious. He had something else in mind for Rolly. A plot so insidious Steve would be the talk of the middle school for years to come.

Drew went directly to the coffin. Rolly could hear something going on out there but couldn't tell what it was. **But we can tell you:** Drew was assembling a dolly. "Hello? Who's out there?" Rolly asked. Drew said nothing, whistling while he worked. He slid the coffin onto the dolly. It weighed a ton, with or without Rolly inside. "Hey! Where are you taking me?" Drew proceeded in silence, wheeling the coffin out to the car park. "Hellooooo! Someone's alive in here!"

**Well, that was the point, wasn't it? That whole 'fate worse than death' thing, as discussed ad nauseam. (Some more Latin for you, foolish reader. It means 'If you say that one more time, I'll vomit'. Loosely translated, of course.)**

To really appreciate the terrors that went on next, you'd have to experience them from Rolly's point of view.

**For some of you, this next section won't be pleasant. But the**

rest of you came for a reason. You've made it past a possessed baseball glove and an enchanted wishbone and an ancient sea beast. You might as well go the distance.

Rolly felt the dolly travelling across gravelly pavement. He could hear the sounds the night makes: the swirling wind along with its friends, the crickets. And then there was a feeling of unsteadiness as the coffin was lifted into a vehicle – a hearse, of course – followed by a short drive. Rolly felt each bump, every turn. Where were they taking him, and for what purpose?

The answer came just moments after the hearse stopped. Then, dread of all dreads: Rolly felt his body being lowered. One, two, three, four, five, six. Six feet under. It had to be a joke, right? *Ha-ha, very funny.* Except for the following sound, which was anything but a punchline.

*Shnnnnk!* What was that?

Oh, nothing much. Just the sound a shovel makes when it enters dirt. Followed by something decidedly worse. Hmm. What could be worse? Try the sound that same dirt makes when it's being dumped onto a coffin – *your coffin* – as you're buried alive!

Forty minutes later, Steve's bike zipped into the car park of the Davis Family Funeral Home. In his left hand was a bag containing a strawberry-banana smoothie – Rolly's consolation prize for being the butt of a pretty sick joke. After he dismounted, Steve noticed an Eternal Rest Deluxe Recliner by a small mound near the construction pit. His cousin hopped out of the hearse and met him halfway across the car park. Steve was eager to hear how it had gone.

"Like a dream, Cuz," Drew replied before reconsidering. "For him, maybe a nightmare." He gave Steve the details. How the coffin had been loaded into the hearse and driven in circles. How he'd lowered it into the construction pit and dumped dirt onto the lid. And – voilà! – buried alive.

**Roland Price wasn't really buried alive. You may breathe, dear reader. For now.**

Steve was barely able to breathe, he was laughing so hard. "Did he scream? Did he say the words 'I quit'?"

Drew thought about it. "Now that you mention it, no. He didn't say anything at all."

"Sure he did." They approached the coffin. "There had to be some begging. Just a little." Again, Drew shook his head. "Not even a whimper?"

"Seriously, dude, he didn't make a peep."

In a fit of temper, Steve threw the smoothie across the

car park, a strawberry-banana *splat*! How was that possible? Was Rolly Price truly unbeatable?

By then, Drew was ready to call it quits. *You win some, you lose some.* He approached the coffin and undid the lock. But before he opened the lid, Steve stuck out his hand. "Wait!" He checked his timer: three more seconds to go. Drew shook his head. "Dude, really?"

Steve nodded. "Three... two... one."

Drew opened the lid and took a step back, allowing his cousin the first look inside. For a moment, Steve didn't know what he was seeing. Or, more accurately, what he *wasn't* seeing. He brushed his hand across the blue velvet interior. "Where is he?" Drew returned to his side and they both stared down, bug-eyed, in silence.

The coffin was empty. Roland Price was gone.

"This is crazy!" shouted Steve. "He's in there somewhere. He has to be!" He frantically examined the coffin – the top, bottom and sides.

"I did everything like we planned!" explained Drew in a panic. "I snatched the coffin from viewing room two, loaded it in the hearse— "

Did you catch that? Because Steve certainly did.

"Wait–wait–wait! Viewing room two. You said 'viewing room two'!"

Drew nodded. "Uh-huh."

"Rolly was in viewing room three. Drew, you took the wrong coffin!"

Drew stood there, teetering in shock. It was like he hadn't heard what he'd just heard. Except he'd heard it! Steve couldn't wait for him to play catch-up. He had to act – fast! Rolly's life might depend on it. He ran back into viewing room three, only to discover an empty platform. "Wh-wh-where's the coffin?" He kicked over a folding chair, collapsing all the chairs like dominoes. "Where did it go?"

Drew arrived seconds later. "They must have taken it."

"Who? Taken it where?"

Drew knew his cousin wasn't going to like the next bit, but he said it anyway. "Where do you think? Where coffins go. To get buried in a cemetery."

"Which one, Drew? Before his air runs out! Which cemetery?"

The look on Drew's face said *I dunno*. "We go everywhere. That's our motto. Mr Davis must have scheduled an after-hours pickup."

"Find out. Call your boss!"

# CHAPTER ELEVEN

Now Drew was on the brink of a full-blown panic attack. "Call my boss? Do you know how serious this is? I can lose my job. Worse than that, I'll go to prison!"

"It doesn't matter! Don't you understand? We locked a kid in a coffin!"

Drew glared at his cousin. He didn't like the implication, not one bit. "No, Cuz. The way I see it, *you* locked a kid in a coffin. All I did was sprinkle a little dirt on an empty box." And on that note, Drew headed to the hearse and settled in behind the wheel.

Steve chased after him, on the verge of begging. Okay, it wasn't the verge. This was a full-on beg fest. "Please-please-please! I'll do anything! You have to help me!" He smushed his face against the windscreen. "It's Steve-o! You can't do this to me!"

"You did it to yourself, kid. We warned you. The whole family warned you! These dares would be the death of you. But you wouldn't listen."

"I'm listening now!" Steve took a breath, then backed away from the windscreen. "I'm listening now."

"Tell that to Rolly. A little... too little, too late – wouldn't you say?" Drew threw the hearse in gear and drove out of the car park, leaving Steve standing alone with nothing but his terrible thoughts. He had to think, to work out his next move. But before he could do that, his phone buzzed with a text. There was a message from Rolly. Steve's hand shook as he stared at the display. It said:

DIG ME UP.

Still, as bad as the text was, Steve was somewhat relieved to know Rolly was alive and breathing, and that was a start. At the same time, he was trapped in a coffin – the Eternal Rest Deluxe Recliner – with about two more hours of air at best.

Steve returned a text, asking Rolly if he knew where they'd taken him. A reply came back almost immediately: HURRY THE WORMS.

That was horrible news. Mostly for Rolly. The worms, they were another story. Logistics-wise, Steve couldn't possibly cover every graveyard in town. He would need help, his first recruit being the always reliable Noah, who Steve thought might still be up, perusing his dad's old horror comics. But Noah texted back: CAN'T – BIGGER FISH TO FRY. At the moment, Noah was attending a pool party. Heh.

Steve was about to try Willa and Tim when it occurred to him: mobile phones are equipped with GPS! He'd be able to pinpoint Rolly's exact location through his phone signal. Several swipes later, he did just that, locating Rolly Price at the Eternal Grace Cemetery, one of the oldest, most distinguished boneyards in the land. All Steve had to do was dig him up, as per Rolly's written request, and they could put this whole misunderstanding behind them.

In theory, anyway.

What would he need? The proper tools, of course. To dig up a grave!

Steve remembered seeing a spade in the garage; thank goodness Mum liked to tinker in the garden. Or maybe she was a gravedigger. **Who knows what mothers do while their children are at school?**

Steve hopped on his bike and was back home within minutes, rummaging through the garage. He located the spade, stuffed it into a bag and was soon gliding back down the driveway when his father stumbled onto the front porch, barely awake. In his underwear. "Yo! Where you goin' with that stuff at this time of night?"

Steve didn't have time to discuss it. "Some dude's buried alive and I have to dig him up!"

His father nodded, never quite opening his eyes. "Okey-doke. Got your house key?"

"Got it!"

His father scratched his butt and headed back inside.

Steve tore across town, topping his best speed. Eternal Grace Cemetery was thirteen miles away, and by the time he arrived, the moon was high in the night sky. It had to be after midnight.

From the outside, the graveyard looked even older than its reputation suggested. There were no street lights, of course, but there was plenty of atmosphere. You know the kind. Leaves rustling in the wind. Creaks, rattles and a familiar *caw-caw* from within a blackened tree. Steve looked up.

A large raven – yes, *that* raven – was perched on a branch, peering down as if to pass judgement.

Steve had to keep moving. Clouds began to pass in front of the moon. It was too dark to wing it *(bad pun intended)*. To compensate, he switched his phone to night vision mode. Moving it back and forth, he picked up an image: there were three dudes hunched together by the side of the road. Hitch-hikers in old-fashioned attire, thumbing for a lift. An unnatural glow pulsated around them – probably a camera defect or a lens flare; Steve couldn't tell which. But when he glanced up to see them 'live', the hitch-hikers were gone.

They must have found a ride. Good for them.

Steve squeezed through the gate, entering the hallowed

ground. As he passed through a forest of crumbling tombstones, Steve knew this was as scared as he'd ever been. Still, for Rolly Price, he had to press on. Passing grave after grave, name after name, song after song. **Yes, the dearly departed do like to sing.**

It was true. Steve could hardly believe it himself. He could have sworn he heard a barbershop quartet harmonising within the graveyard. Steve looked through his phone again to see in night vision, and the sight that met his eyes was beyond his darkest imaginings. The Eternal Grace Cemetery was alive with movement and song in a *gore*geous panorama of macabre merriment; phantasms of every size, shape and denomination had manifested everywhere!

To protect his own sanity, Steve decided it was a dream – it had to be – albeit a magical one. And if it was a dream, maybe the whole Rolly Price incident had never happened. He could wake up and start the day all over again. But a new text from Rolly guillotined that happy thought. This one simply said: FASTER NO AIR.

Steve switched back to GPS mode, rendering the graveyard lifeless once more. At least, to the naked eye. A tiny flag on the display indicated YOU ARE HERE. *Here* happened to be the site of a fresh grave without a headstone. Those come later.

For the time being, it was just a big ole pile of dirt. And six feet under that dirt was Rolly Price, snug inside the Eternal Rest Deluxe Recliner. Guaranteed not to rot for ten years.

Steve pulled the spade from his bag. "Hang in there, Roll. I'm coming!" He began to dig, dig, dig, spraying dirt into the air like somebody's life depended on it – which it did. Before long, Steve was in the grave, digging as fast as he could until – *THWACK!* Steve hit coffin, then cleared away the layer of soil on top by hand, worms squishing between his fingers. "Almost there, buddy boy!"

Soon there was only the lock to deal with. Steve used the spade, splitting it in two. *You can forget about that ten-year guarantee.* He slid his fingers under the lid and, in the millisecond before it opened, thought about what he might find inside. The blue velvet interior would likely be shredded, with bits of Rolly's fingernails embedded in the lining. And what of Rolly himself? As he'd tried to escape, his frustration might have led to insanity. He would be a foaming mad lunatic; his only thoughts would be acts of vengeance... against ole Steve-o himself.

But whatever the outcome, Steve had accepted his fate. For it was a fate of his own design. His hands clasped the lid, opening the coffin in silence. (You can forget those surround-sound *creeeeeaks* you hear in the movies.) "Roll?" enquired Steve, really hoping he wouldn't get a reply from anyone other than Rolly. But Steve's real fear was getting no response at all, which was what happened. He clicked on his torch app and looked inside.

Steve almost fainted when he saw the body, and he had to use the walls of the grave to keep himself from collapsing. There was, as he'd feared, a stiffened corpse inside the coffin, its face an unnatural blend of blues and greens. The eyes, which had retreated into the back of the skull, were a milky white. What had Steve done? How much had his dares cost him?

He leant in, eyeball-to-eyeball with the lifeless shell of his former rival. There wasn't much he could say. *Sorry I buried you alive?* Well, that would be a start. But in fact, the first word to emerge from Steve's mouth was... "Marshmallows?" He had got a good look at the eyes and that was exactly what they were. At the same time, he recognised the face from Parties 4 Smarties. It was a Halloween mask.

Steve had been played, big time. But *how*?

Before he could cry out in madness – and I am delighted to inform you, that is coming – he heard the sound of a phone... this time not his own. Steve looked around, finding it by his feet in the corpse's pipe-cleaner hand. He plucked the phone loose and, with all the craziness swirling around him, managed a demure "Hello?"

A voice on the other end exploded with laughter. "Lost again, Steve-o!" Yes, it was Roland Price.

Steve squeezed the phone, about to crush it as he would have crushed Rolly, given the chance. The complete and utter humiliation. The remarks he would have to endure at school! But all he could hear then was Rolly laughing his guts out.

"It was your cousin!" Rolly started to explain. "The Drew-meister! The entire shebang was his idea. He said you needed to learn your lesson, once and for all, about the price of all those dares. Well, have you?" Rolly had to stop talking, because from that point on, all he could manage was *"Ha-ha-ha-ha-ha!"*

Yet Steve wasn't in on the joke. No, not that time. His eyes, the same ones the girls usually swooned over, had turned to stone. And his smile was no longer roguish. Now it was wide – a little too wide. As if Steve had gone totally insane.

"Double dare!" he blurted into the phone, invoking the next rule of the game. "All I have to do is last two little hours inside this coffin and I get my title back! Who's shaking now, buddy boy?"

It might have been a rhetorical question, but as it turned out, Rolly really was shaking. He had heard the change in Steve's voice. It was the verbal equivalent of that mad smile, and it scared the laugh right out of him. "Okay, Steve, enough is enough. Joke's over. What are you doing?"

"Taking a little nap. Wake me when I get my title back." Steve climbed into the coffin, lying on top of the dummy corpse. It was additional padding – not that the Eternal Rest Deluxe Recliner needed it. And anyway, if Steve got hungry, he could always eat the eyeballs.

Rolly was still pleading when Steve clicked off the phone and lowered the lid. Now his world was dark but far from silent. Because Steve was still rambling for all the nearby apparitions to hear. "Come Monday, I'll be king again. All hail the king of dares!"

By then, total exhaustion had settled in. It had been quite an evening, filled with searching… and worrying… and digging. So Steve closed his eyes and took a nap, just like he'd said he would. Soon he fell into a deep slumber. He didn't even stir when a caretaker, accompanied by his shivering bloodhound, wandered by the open grave and, using the same spade Steve had left behind, shovelled the remaining dirt over the Eternal Rest Deluxe Recliner, burying him alive.

By the time Rolly convinced the sheriff to excavate the grave, more than four hours had gone by. When they finally opened the coffin, they found Steve with his arms folded across his chest, looking positively regal. His oxygen had expired, accounting for the royal-blue hue. And unless Rolly was imagining it, he noticed that Steve's lips were curled, indicating total satisfaction. The corpse in the casket was filled with pride – and more than a few worms. Rolly Price was forced to concede. Ole Steve-o was once again the king of dares… for all eternity.

# Chapter Twelve

The librarian closed the book. But don't you, dear reader. You still have several pages to go.

His Royal Highness, King Steve-o himself, was now back in the library, surrounded by his best buds. Yet there was no comfort. No warmth. Like his friends, he felt only the chill of the grave. This time, the librarian didn't ask for criticisms or comments. He knew from the group's frosty expressions that the time for commentary had passed. "Now do I get my ice cream?"

Steve's hands balled into fists, but not from anger; he was just trying to conceal the dirt under his nails. "No, you don't get your ice cream! That was the least scary of them all! Now you said we could leave, old man." Steve puffed out his chest, as if that might intimidate a talking skull. "Let us leave – right now – or there'll be trouble."

"Allow you to leave?" The librarian seemed puzzled. "There's been a *grave* misunderstanding. You may come and go as you please – all of you. This is your home, after all. Your happy haunt. Forever."

"What's going on?" demanded Steve, looking at the others. "What's he talking about?"

Willa was the first to piece it together. "Those tales he read. Our stories. Each one ended with the main character…"

"Dying…" the librarian paused, "… to know what happens next."

Noah asked, "What *does* happen next?"

As if to respond, the book left the librarian's hand and floated purposefully to its space on the shelf. Other books began to vibrate, growing giddy with excitement. They had their own tales they wanted to share.

"The spirits are indeed playful this evening," the librarian said. "They can hardly contain themselves."

And so they were. Volumes of ghost stories began floating across the library. The happy haunts had received their sympathetic vibrations and were beginning to materialise.

# CHAPTER TWELVE

The group could hardly believe their eyes. All manner of spirits appeared – young, old, tall, short – all carrying the books that contained their tales. And that was the least of it!

Willa pointed at Tim. "Timothy! What do you think you're doing? You know better than to come apart at the seams!"

But Tim couldn't help himself. His parts had detached from his torso and were now drifting independently throughout the library, in the same order as Lefty had dismantled them. Tim's floating head noticed a change in Willa, too. "That's pretty gnarly, Will," he said, hovering above. "Pretty gnarly."

"What are you talking about?" Willa looked down at her arm and saw the real-life chompings of a rabbit, a parrot and a goldfish. Her flesh was riddled with bite marks.

What about Steve? He was still in one piece, thank goodness, but his complexion was blue, as if he'd been holding his breath for hours... days... weeks... years. And yet he still looked cooler than Noah, who was blowing about five hundred gallons of salt water from his nose – and loving every minute of it.

In that moment, the Fearsome Foursome understood. They too, were spirits, spectres, poltergeists, apparitions. Or, if you prefer...

... ghosts.

Their ethereal forms took flight, joining the other spirits in their midst. Music swept in from beyond the bookshelves. The party was just getting started, and Willa so wanted to join in. "Let's go, Tim-bo. Take me dancing." She took Tim's hand and floated through the wall in search of the ballroom. A moment later, the rest of Tim's parts followed. But not Noah and Steve. They flew off to cause some mischief in the graveyard.

For the Fearsome Foursome, a new and wondrous adventure had begun. For they were the newest residents of the happiest haunt on earth.

# Here after Thoughts

Some final words of discomfort
before you turn out the lights...

You didn't heed our warning.
You stayed until the bitter end.

Maybe I misjudged you.
Maybe you are our type.
As I said, every spirit has a story.
Share yours, won't you?
I've cleared a space up on my bookshelf.
You are cordially invited to remain with
us for all eternity.

Welcome, foolish reader.
Welcome to the Haunted Mansion.

# BIOGRAPHIES

**Amicus Arcane** *Little is known about the dearly departed Amicus Arcane, save for his love of books. As the mansion librarian, both in this life and in the afterlife, Amicus has delighted in all forms of the written word. However, this librarian's favourite tales are those of terror and suspense. After all, there is nothing better to ease a restless spirit than a frightfully good ghost story.*

**John Esposito** *When John Esposito met Amicus Arcane on a midnight stroll through New Orleans Square, he was so haunted by the librarian's tales that he decided to transcribe them for posterity. John has worked in both film and television, on projects such as* Stephen King's Graveyard Shift, R. L. Stine's The Haunting Hour, Teen Titans *and the* Walking Dead *web series, for which he won consecutive Writer's Guild Awards. John lives in New York with his wife and children and still visits with Amicus from time to time.*

**Kelley Jones** *For the illustrations accompanying his terrifying tales, Amicus Arcane approached Kelley Jones, an artist with a scary amount of talent. Kelley has worked for every major comic book publisher, but is best known for his definitive work on Batman for DC Comics. Kelley lives in Northern California with his wife and children and hears from Amicus every October 31, whether he wants to or not.*

DEAD END!

Prepare to exit
to the Living World